Beyond The Path
True Tales of Terror in the Woods

Volume 1

Erik Lake

FREE REIGN

Contents

ONE

A LEGENDARY CREATURE

In the autumn of 1966, before the world had ever heard the name "Mothman," I found myself in the small town of Point Pleasant, West Virginia. It was a sleepy, picturesque community nestled on the banks of the Ohio River, surrounded by dense woods that seemed to stretch on forever. Little did I know that my stay there would forever be marked by a chilling encounter that defied explanation. I had traveled to Point Pleasant on business, and my work took me to the outskirts of town where the woods loomed ominously. My appointment had run late, and as the sun dipped below the horizon, casting long shadows through the trees, I found myself on a lonely road that led into the heart of the forest. The woods were thick with the crisp, sweet scent of autumn leaves, and the only sounds were the distant hum of a car engine and the gentle whisper of the wind through the trees. As I drove deeper into the woods, I couldn't shake the feeling that I was being watched. Despite the chill in the air, I had rolled down my driver side window to let some air into my vehicle. The rustling of leaves underneath my car's tires and the eerie silence of the forest sent shivers down my spine. It was starting to give me the creeps and I started thinking about all the horror and science fiction stories I had read as a little kid. I chided myself for letting my imagination get the best of me. It was just a forest, after all. I laughed and reminded myself that it was just a lonely road traveling through a forest and my senses were on high alert due to the fact that I was from a much blogger city halfway across the country and it was an unusual sort of path to have to travel in the dark.

However, as I rounded a bend in the road, I saw something that defied all reason. At first, it was just a fleeting glimpse, a shadowy figure darting between the trees. I slammed on the brakes, heart pounding in my chest, and stepped out of the car, straining to see through the gathering darkness. I didn't have a flashlight but I didn't need one as the high beams from my car were more than sufficient to light up the area around me. I looked all over the place, but mainly I scanned in the direction where I had seen the dark figure running towards. I looked up and couldn't believe what I was seeing. There, in the dim light, I saw it—a towering, winged figure perched on a distant tree branch. It was crouched down but I could tell it could stand bipedally, like a human being does. Its eyes, like two fiery orbs, glowed with an eerie red light that pierced right through the darkness of the night. My breath caught in my throat, and I stood there, frozen in terror, as the creature unfurled its immense wings and took flight. It was like no bird I had ever seen. Its wingspan stretched at least ten feet, and its body seemed to be covered in a dark, leathery hide. The wings beat with a strange, rhythmic cadence, and it rose into the air with an uncanny grace. I could hardly believe my eyes. This was the creature I had heard the locals in the diner that morning whispering about—the Mothman. I remember eavesdropping on them and getting a kick out of how ridiculous, and how serious, they sounded.

My heart raced and my mind immediately went to the camera I had in my glove compartment in the car. However, before I could even turn and start running back to the car, the Mothman had disappeared into the night, leaving me with nothing but a chilling photograph of the dark forest. Shaken to my core, I made a hasty retreat from that desolate stretch of road. The events of that evening haunted my dreams, and I found myself unable to concentrate on my work. The legend of the Mothman was well known in Point Pleasant, and I soon found myself drawn into the town's growing obsession with the creature. I began to research the history of the Mothman and discovered that sightings had been reported throughout the area for over a year. Local newspapers were filled with accounts of witnesses who had encountered the creature in the woods, near the old TNT plant, and even in their own backyards. The descriptions were eerily consistent—an enormous, bipedal, winged figure with glowing red eyes. The more I delved into the lore of the Mothman, the more I realized that my own encounter was not an isolated incident. Some believed that the creature was a harbinger of doom, a malevolent omen that foretold tragic events. This idea gained disturbing credibility when, just over a year after my sighting, tragedy struck Point Pleasant.

On December 15, 1967, which was only about fourteen months after I had been there and had my sighting, the Silver Bridge, a vital link connecting Point Pleasant to Gallipolis, Ohio, collapsed during rush hour, sending dozens of cars and their occupants plunging into the icy waters of the Ohio River. The disaster claimed the lives of 46 people, and it was a moment of unspeakable horror for the town. As I watched the news coverage of the bridge collapse, a cold sweat broke out on my brow. The Mothman sightings had been eerily predictive of the tragedy, and I couldn't help but feel a profound sense of unease. Was it all a coincidence, or was the Mothman somehow connected to the disaster? In the years that followed, I would often find myself drawn back to Point Pleasant, unable to escape the shadow of that fateful encounter. The legend of the Mothman endured, and a sense of foreboding clung to the town. Some believed that the creature was a guardian, a protector of Point Pleasant, while others feared it as a malevolent force. No matter the interpretation, the Mothman had left an indelible mark on the town's history, and its legend continued to grow. It became a source of fascination and dread, a symbol of the unknown and the unexplained. It also made me wonder and worry if perhaps something terrible would befall me, specifically, since I had also seen it and it seemed at that time to actually be the harbinger of doom and disaster most people thought that it was.

To this day, I can't say for certain what I witnessed in those West Virginia woods but I'm 99.9 percent sure that it was the mothman. I mean, what else could it have been? The Mothman remains a mystery, an enigma that defies explanation. But one thing is clear: that chance encounter changed the course of my life, and I will forever carry the memory of those glowing red eyes and dark wings with me, a reminder that some mysteries are never meant to be solved. As the years passed, Point Pleasant embraced its notoriety as the home of the Mothman, and the town erected a statue in honor of the enigmatic creature. The statue stood tall in the center of town, its wings outstretched and its eyes aglow, a testament to the enduring fascination with the legend. Visitors from far and wide flocked to Point Pleasant, eager to hear the tales of the Mothman and to witness the place where it all began. The town's annual Mothman Festival became a beloved tradition, with vendors selling everything from Mothman-themed merchandise to local delicacies. For me, the annual pilgrimage to Point Pleasant became a personal tradition. Each year, I returned to the town that had left an indelible mark on my life, and I couldn't help but feel a sense of reverence for the Mothman. Whether guardian or harbinger, the creature had become a part of the town's identity, a symbol of the inexplicable.

Whenever I would go back to Point Pleasant I would often find myself wandering through the woods that had once been the setting of my own encounter with the Mothman. The forest had an eerie beauty, especially in the waning light of the day, when the leaves rustled with secrets and the air seemed to carry a whisper of something otherworldly. One evening, as I ventured deeper into the woods, I came across an old, dilapidated structure hidden among the trees—the remnants of the infamous TNT plant that had been associated with the Mothman sightings. The abandoned bunkers and storage buildings bore silent witness to a bygone era when the area had been a hub of wartime activity. The setting was undeniably eerie, and I couldn't help but wonder if this place had played a role in the legend of the Mothman. The stories of strange lights, unexplained noises, and eerie encounters at the TNT plant had only added to the aura of mystery that surrounded the creature. As I explored the ruins, a sudden chill gripped me, and I felt as though I were being watched once again. I turned my gaze to the surrounding trees, scanning the shadows for any sign of movement. It was at that moment that I heard it—the faint, rhythmic sound of wings. My heart quickened as I looked up into the trees, and there, perched on a gnarled branch, was the unmistakable figure of the Mothman. Its wings beat with an uncanny grace, and its eyes glowed with an eerie intensity, fixed on me with an unblinking gaze.

I fumbled for my camera, which at that time I had been smart enough to put in my pocket just in case I saw anything, but not really expecting to, which is why I didn't have it in my hands or more readily accessible. I had been determined to capture the creature on film but was once again thwarted in my attempt to do so. Just as before, before I could barely form a coherent thought about the camera and snapping some photos, the Mothman vanished into the night, leaving me with nothing more than the haunting memory of those glowing red eyes and dark wings. It was just like the last time I had come face to face with the now legendary creature. The encounter left me shaken, but it also left me with a sense of wonder and a deepening fascination with the legend of the Mothman. I couldn't help but wonder if the creature was a guardian of the forest, a silent sentinel of the unknown. In the years that followed, I continued to visit Point Pleasant, and I still go there at least once a year, more if I can manage it. I'm drawn back by the allure of the Mothman and the enigmatic woods that had been the setting of both of my encounters. I speak with locals who have their own tales to tell, and I listen to the stories of those who believe that the Mothman is a protector, a sort of guardian of the town. Some claim that the creature has saved them from accidents or guided them through dangerous situations. Others see it as a symbol of hope and resilience in the face of tragedy. The Mothman has become a source of inspiration, a reminder that even in the darkest of times, there is a glimmer of light. As the decades pass, the legend of the Mothman continues to grow, and Point Pleasant remains its heart. The town has embraced its unique place in history, and the Mothman has become an enduring symbol of the inexplicable. To this day, I can't say for certain what the Mothman is or what it represents. But I do know that the creature has left an indelible mark on my life, and on the lives of so many others, especially those who are local to where the Silver Bridge tragedy took place. It more than likely will forever remain a reminder that there are mysteries in this world that defy explanation. It is a testament to the enduring power of the unknown, and the haunting beauty of the unexplained.

Two
Translucent Humanoid Encounter

In the summer of 1979, four of my friends and I, all between the ages of twenty one and twenty three, embarked on a journey that would forever change the way we viewed our world. The remote and densely forested wilderness of Lake Serenity was to be our sanctuary, a place where we could escape the mundane world and seek adventure. But what we encountered in those dark woods was far beyond our wildest imagination, a chilling entity that would etch itself into our memories with an intensity that defied belief. I'm changing all of our names to protect those of us who don't want to talk about what happened to us. The members of our group consisted of Mark, a rugged outdoorsman with a penchant for tall tales; Lisa, the bookish and inquisitive one with an uncanny ability to see the extraordinary in the ordinary; Mike, an adrenaline junkie who lived for the thrill of the unknown; Jenny, my steadfast and no-nonsense best friend, always the voice of reason; and I'm Sara. I've always had a fascination with the unexplained and the supernatural. As we approached that remote, densely wooded forest in which the lake was located one late summer evening, none of us could have foreseen the terror that awaited us. The air was thick with anticipation, and the sound of our laughter and cracking sticks underfoot was soon overshadowed by the ominous rustling of the trees. We were young and adventurous, seeking a thrill, and we found it that night – an encounter with an entity that defied explanation. The place we had chosen for our weekend retreat was Lake Serenity, nestled deep within a vast and impenetrable forest. It was a place only whispered about in local legends, and few dared to venture into its heart. Our group consisted of five friends, all in our early twenties, bound by our shared desire for adventure and a touch of recklessness. I, Sarah, recount this story from my perspective, but I was not alone in witnessing the inexplicable.

The journey to Lake Serenity was fraught with difficulty, but the allure of isolation and untouched beauty was too enticing to resist. We were only planning on being there for a few days, but we had packed enough food, tents, and camping gear to survive a month. As we trekked through the dense woods, the oppressive canopy of trees and the enigmatic darkness beneath only fueled our excitement. Upon reaching the lake, we set up our campsite. The moon shone brightly in the clear, starry sky, casting an eerie, shimmering light over the water. We gathered around the campfire, its crackling flames creating dancing shadows, and told stories to stave off the mounting unease. It was during that initial camaraderie that we first heard it – the faint, strange clicking noises that seemed to emanate from the surrounding forest. It was as if some otherworldly presence was trying to communicate with us. Naturally, we assumed it was some forest creature or a peculiar insect, and we tried to dismiss the unnerving sounds. But the clicking grew louder, more rhythmic, and hauntingly distinct. The night air seemed to quiver with anticipation, and the unease that initially bubbled up in us now turned into a collective sense of dread that was unlike any of us had ever experienced before.

As we huddled together around the fire, our eyes were drawn to the lake, and there, from the inky depths, a phenomenon both horrifying and captivating began to emerge. It was an entity that defied the laws of nature. In the moonlight, it shimmered and rippled like a mirage. The entity appeared translucent, like a ghostly figure hovering just above the water's surface. It was at that moment that I realized this entity was invisible unless it was wet. As it climbed out of the lake, it was soaked and held its shape, a grotesque yet mesmerizing form. We were speechless, unable to comprehend the reality of what we were witnessing. The entity stood there, glistening, and undulating in the moonlight, its body elongated and vaguely humanoid. Years later I would see a movie called The Predator and I recognized the movie's villain, the entity in the movie, immediately as what we saw at the lake that night. It was as if it was composed of water, taking on the properties of its surroundings. The clicking noises it made were now louder, more pronounced, and resembled an eerie language or communication. It was both fascinating and terrifying. The entity seemed aware of our presence, and our fear grew as we realized it was coming closer to our campfire. Our curiosity was overtaken by an instinctual need to flee, but our legs felt like lead. We were paralyzed by a mixture of awe and terror. I don't think as it approached the creature, or whatever it was, knew we had spotted it or that we were able to see it at all. We all just sat there staring at it, unable to move but desperately wanting to run and never look back.

My friend Mark was the first to break free from the paralyzing fear. In a panic, he grabbed a nearby bucket of water and flung it at the entity. As the water hit it, the entity momentarily solidified, revealing its grotesque form. The moonlight played off its surface, making it appear even more otherworldly. It let out a series of violent sounding clicks and retreated back into the lake, vanishing into the dark water. The shimmering form dissipated, leaving us in silence. We spent a restless night, our campfire dwindling to embers, keeping a watchful eye on the lake. We had witnessed something beyond our comprehension, an entity that seemed to belong to another realm. None of us dared to enter the lake, knowing that it was the domain of the otherworldly entity and who even knew what else. Morning finally broke, and with the first light of dawn, we made a hasty retreat from Lake Serenity. The eerie memory of the entity and its clicking language haunted us as we navigated the dense forest, our steps heavy with trepidation. We emerged from the woods, our story one that we would share with others, though it would be met with skepticism and disbelief. We all survived our encounter with the entity, but the experience left us forever changed. The remote, dense forest had revealed a secret that we were not meant to know, an entity beyond our understanding.

To this day, I cannot explain what we witnessed at Lake Serenity. It remains a chilling and unexplainable memory that I sometimes wonder if my mind made it up and if it never actually happened. It feels like I've lost my mind sometimes. It's a complete and total mystery; an encounter with the unknown that lingers in the back of my mind constantly. I often find myself listening for the faint clicking noises in the night, wondering if the entity we saw still dwells in that remote and forbidding place or if it somehow left those woods and is waiting for the right moment to strike out and finish what it started with me and my friends so long ago. Remember, it had been approaching us, more than likely unaware we were even aware of its presence and I often wonder what its intentions were, knowing all the same that they weren't in any way, shape or form good and honorable. It serves as a reminder that the world is vast and filled with mysteries, some of which are better left undisturbed. It's a memory that, to this day, sends shivers down my spine. The entity itself, its origin and purpose, remain shrouded in mystery, and it is difficult to categorize it as anything other than an unexplained enigma. Even seeing it in that movie back in the eighties didn't lend much explanation as to its true nature or what we were really dealing with. That was only a movie. It did, however, at least let me know that someone, somewhere knew about it. There's no way possible that someone just happened to come up with that thing out of the clear blue sky, pulling it from the depths of a creative imagination and whether they know it or not, I'm convinced whoever made that movie saw the entity somewhere, at some point and either did or didn't know it.

The days and weeks that followed our escape from Lake Serenity were filled with a sense of disbelief and lingering fear. We tried to rationalize what we had witnessed. Some suggested it was a creature from the depths of the lake, others thought it might be an extraterrestrial being, and a few even considered it an ancient spirit guarding a long-forgotten secret. Regardless of its nature, one thing was clear: the entity gave off an overwhelming sense of malevolence. The clicking noises that echoed through the forest were not merely sounds but conveyed a presence of pure evil, an entity that existed beyond the realm of our understanding. It was as if we had encountered a force that had no regard for the laws of our world. The forest, once buzzing with the sounds of nature, had fallen silent in the wake of the entity's appearance. It was as if the very woods themselves held their breath, awaiting the next move of this supernatural interloper. In the days that followed, we couldn't shake the feeling that the entity was not finished with us. Some of us even thought we had seen it, its glistening form lurking in the shadows of the trees wherever we were. Others believed that it had followed us, a silent and unseen presence that watched our every move. We became increasingly paranoid, our bonds of friendship strained by the shared trauma of our encounter. We decided to seek answers, consulting local legends, and speaking with experts in the fields of the paranormal and cryptozoology. While we found no definitive explanations for what we had experienced, we did discover that Lake Serenity had a history of strange occurrences and sightings dating back centuries.

One story we uncovered spoke of a mysterious tribe that had inhabited the area long before settlers arrived. According to legend, the tribe had worshiped a water deity, which they believed could take on various forms, including that of a shimmering, shape-shifting entity. The entity was said to possess knowledge of both the past and the future, and it was invoked during sacred ceremonies. Could the entity we encountered be a remnant of this ancient belief? Or was it something else entirely, a being that had chosen this secluded lake as its home for reasons unknown to us? Our search for answers only led to more questions, and we realized that some mysteries are meant to remain unsolved. The entity at Lake Serenity had left an indelible mark on our lives, possibly even our souls too, forever altering our perceptions of reality and the supernatural. In the years that followed, we went our separate ways, each of us haunted by the memory of that fateful night. Lake Serenity remained an untouched, unexplored realm, a place of unsolved mysteries and inexplicable phenomena. It's not that dozens of people or more don't visit there every year, it's just that most of them don't even know what they're sharing the lake with and honestly it makes me wonder what else is out there, lurking in those woods that are so vast and dense that no one would have heard us scream should we have been able to do so. And so, the tale of the entity at Lake Serenity continues to be whispered among those who dare to venture into the remote, densely wooded wilderness. It serves as a chilling reminder that the world is vast and filled with mysteries that elude our understanding. The entity, with its eerie clicking language and malevolent presence, remains a testament to the inexplicable forces that lurk in the depths of the unknown. It is a story that we will carry with us to the end of our days, a memory that defies explanation and endures as a chilling enigma in our lives.

THREE
REPTILIAN ABDUCTION

I didn't decide to talk about my experience publicly, in this encounter story, because I care at all if people believe me. I did it so that people who have experienced something similar but are too afraid to talk about it for fear of being ridiculed can know they aren't alone. I was visiting some family for a wedding in Florida and decided to stay the weekend but not with the wedding party or the rest of my family and friends who were there. I overheard some people at the wedding discussing an allegedly haunted area of woods that was about an hour away and I was immediately interested in checking it out. I had to rearrange my flight but that was simple enough. I told everyone what I planned on doing and though some warned me not to go out into those woods, most of the people there who knew me well knew that I wasn't going to be deterred. I explored all different forests and wood-lands every chance I got and have even been to some allegedly haunted woods in other countries as well. My wife, who had stayed at home with our newborn daughter, was understanding as she chuckled and told me to be careful and make sure that I was back in time for work on Monday. That's all she cared about. I woke up on Friday, the day after the wedding, and immediately took off to gather the supplies I would need for a weekend in the woods. It was before there was anything I would have been able to really record or document my experiences with that would have been available to the general public, but I didn't expect to see anything anyway. I had been exploring allegedly haunted woods for as long as I could remember at that time and never witnessed or came across anything I couldn't rationally explain away. I had no idea what I was getting myself into. I rented a Jeep that I could take out into the forest with me and headed on my way.

In the darkness of the woods, I embarked on a journey, drawn by the allure of the mysterious and the unknown. Forests always seemed like such sanctuaries during the daylight hours, but they always seemed to transform into an enigmatic realm after sunset. Guided by the silvery light of the moon, I stepped into a world where my senses buzzed with anticipation, each rustling leaf and nocturnal creature enhancing the thrill of the night. My fascination with the wonders of the natural world and the unnatural things that allegedly haunted it had led me to this remote corner of the forest, known for its unique ecosystem. The region was home to swamps, wetlands, and lush under-growth teeming with life. Armed with a camera, notebook, and a trusty flashlight, I ventured into the heart of the wilderness. The symphony of the night filled the air, from the rhythmic chirping of crickets to the melodious croaking of frogs in the nearby swamp. I captured the serene beauty of the nocturnal world with my camera, already gathering images of owls, raccoons, and other elusive creatures. Excitement coursed through me, propelling me forward with every step. The swamp, a few miles away, beckoned to me. Its murky waters and hidden inhabitants held a mystique that I couldn't resist exploring. The moon's reflection on the stagnant surface created an eerie ambiance, casting haunting shadows that seemed to dance in the moonlight. I stood at the swamp's edge, eager to document the unique life that called it home.

As I ventured further into the swamp, my flashlight cast an eerie glow on the still water. The chorus of frogs grew louder, a cacophony of croaks and chirps that filled the night. My senses were immersed in the swamp's ambi-ence, so much so that I didn't immediately notice the strange rustling in the underbrush. My heart quickened as I focused my flashlight on the source of the noise. I froze as the beam of light revealed a bizarre figure a mere few feet away. My breath caught in my throat, and a chill ran down my spine as I locked eyes with the creature. It stood at least six feet tall, its body covered in glistening, greenish-brown scales. Its eyes, large and almond-shaped, held vertical pupils that gleamed in the flashlight's beam. The creature had a long, forked tongue that flickered in and out of its mouth, sampling the air. The creature's limbs were muscular and reptilian, adorned with webbed fingers and toes. A snake-like tail slithered behind it. Its elongated head bore small, bony ridges that ran down its back. This was a sight I couldn't comprehend—a reptilian humanoid being, a creature unlike any I had ever encountered. I attempted to back away slowly, but the creature's gaze never left me. It let out a low, guttural hiss and took a step closer. I stumbled backward, my flashlight trembling as panic surged through me. I turned and ran, pushing through the underbrush. The creature was in pursuit, its hisses growing louder as it gained ground. The forest, once a haven of wonder, had transformed into a labyrinth of terror. My flashlight's beam darted wildly, illuminating the menacing presence behind me.

The woods seemed to be in on it somehow. Branches reached out, clawing at my skin, and roots seemed to purposely try to trip me. The creature's claws scraped against the ground, a constant, menacing force following my every move. It had been bipedal when I had first seen it and it had given chase but now it was on all fours and moving at a supernatural and inhuman speed. Breathless and terrified, I burst through a thicket and into a small clearing. The moonlight filtered through the trees, revealing a sight that sent fresh waves of terror through me. Above the clearing, a dark, saucer-shaped object hung in the night sky—an inexplicable UFO. Its surface rippled with an otherworldly energy, and I couldn't look away. My heart raced as I took in the surreal sight. The UFO was not alone; the reptilian creature had cornered me in the clearing. Its yellow eyes bore into me, its predatory intensity unmistakable. I was trapped, with no way out. The forest seemed to hold its breath, as though nature itself awaited the climax of this bizarre encounter. In the silence, I heard a distant hum emanating from the hovering UFO. The creature, now back standing on its hind legs and upright like a human being, took a step closer, its forked tongue flickering. Its malevolence was palpable, an ancient instinct to dominate and hunt. With no escape, I braced for what was to come. With a deafening roar, the UFO shot skyward, leaving a trail of blazing light. The reptilian creature hissed in frustration; its gaze locked on the vanishing craft. Seizing the opportunity, I turned and fled, putting as much distance as possible between us.

I raced through the woods, the fear and adrenaline

driving me on. The forest seemed to stretch endlessly, and I ran until my legs ached and my lungs burned. Eventually, I collapsed at the edge of a small stream, where the moonlight cast a serene glow on the water's surface. As I caught my breath, I realized I had escaped the clutches of the reptilian humanoid and the UFO. My camera and flashlight were lost, but I carried an unforgettable tale—a night in the wilderness, etched in my memory as a terrifying, otherworldly experience, a brush with the unknown that had forever changed my perception of the natural world. With trembling legs, I continued my escape through the woods, unsure of what other horrors the night held. My mind still reeled from the surreal encounter, and the sound of my own rapid breath served as a constant reminder of the horrors that lurked just beyond the shadows. The hours passed slowly, and I struggled to stay awake, my exhaustion threatening to pull me into slumber. But I knew that if I closed my eyes, I might awaken to a nightmare far worse than any I had experienced before. When I first saw the old, decrepit looking cabin, I thought it was just a mirage or some other thing my exhausted and overwhelmed mind had conjured up. Then I remembered the stories the people at the wedding were telling, about an old, abandoned cabin with broken windows seemingly being the hub of paranormal activity that branched itself out into the forest itself. It wasn't a figment of my imagination at all and I excitedly went inside, immediately barricading the door with whatever I could find.

I wasn't even thinking about the tales of paranormal beings, ghosts, and other entities I had listened to all night long the night before and was just happy to have a place to stay where I at the very least didn't feel so very exposed to the elements, to the darkness or to that Godforsaken creature anymore. I was still terrified but I was also exhausted and I laid my sleeping bag down on the dirty floor and tried to at least get some rest. I planned on making haste out of that forest forever and never returning as soon as the sun began to rise. Just as I was beginning to doze off, a strange sound broke the silence. It was a faint, rhythmic humming that seemed to emanate from the forest outside. I strained my ears to listen, and the sound grew louder, filling the cabin with an otherworldly vibration. I moved closer to one of the broken windows, peering out into the night. My heart raced as I witnessed a sight that defied explanation. The UFO, the same one I had seen earlier, hovered above the cabin, casting an eerie, pulsating light that bathed the surrounding trees in an unnatural glow. The cabin's walls trembled, and the ground beneath me seemed to shake. It was as if the very fabric of reality was being warped by the presence of the UFO. My fear reached new heights as I realized that I was not alone in this encounter, that the inexplicable events of the night were far from over. The UFO's hum intensified, and a strange, otherworldly force seemed to pull at me, as if it were beckoning me to step outside. The cabin's walls groaned under the strain, and I knew that I had no choice but to confront whatever awaited me. With trembling legs, I made my way to the door, moved everything I had piled in front of it and pushed it open. The moonlit forest seemed both familiar and alien, bathed in the surreal light of the hovering craft. I took a hesitant step forward, and the moment my foot touched the ground, a blinding flash of light engulfed me.

A bright light blinded and confused me. It was beaming down on me from up above in the sky and I felt like I was going to pass out. The next thing I knew, I was no longer in the woods. I was inside the UFO, surrounded by a strange, metallic interior that seemed to defy the laws of physics. I was suspended in mid-air, weightless, and my heart raced as I realized that I was not alone. In the dim, pulsating light of the UFO, I saw them—more reptilian humanoid beings, standing in a circle around me. They were different from the one I had encountered earlier, with variations in their scales and features. Their eyes locked onto mine, and I felt a surge of overwhelming dread. One of the beings approached me, its hisses and guttural sounds filling the chamber. It reached out a webbed hand, and I couldn't help but recoil in fear. I was at the mercy of these enigmatic creatures, and I had no way to comprehend their intentions. The being extended its hand once more, but this time, it held a small, metallic device. It pointed the device at me, and a series of strange symbols and images flickered on its surface. I could feel a strange sensation wash over me, as if my very thoughts and memories were being probed. The encounter felt like an eternity, but eventually, the beings stepped back and returned to their circle. The room began to spin, and I felt weightless once more as the world outside the UFO came back into view.

I found myself back in the cabin in the woods, the UFO soaring into the night sky and disappearing from sight. My body ached, and my mind was a whirlwind of confusion and terror. The events of the night had pushed the boundaries of my understanding, and I was left with more questions than answers. Exhausted and shaken to my core, I slept until sunrise and then I made my way out of the woods and back to civilization. I knew that no one would believe the incredible tale I had to tell, and I questioned my own sanity. The mysteries of the natural world had shown me a side of reality I could never have imagined, and the encounter with the unknown would haunt me for the rest of my days. When the sun finally came up I wrote everything down in a small notebook I kept in my backpack when on my forest adventures, because a part of me thought I would somehow forget it or something.

With my story documented, I could only hope that one day the truth behind that fateful night would be uncovered. The woods held their secrets, and the reptilian humanoid beings and the UFO remained enigmatic, leaving me with an enduring sense of wonder and dread. As I finally reached the safety of my home, I couldn't help but look back at the woods with a mix of fear and fascination. The mysteries of the night had left an indelible mark on my soul, a reminder that the natural world was a place of wonder and terror, where the boundaries of reality were ever shifting, and where the unknown could be just beyond the next bend in the path.

FOUR
THE FAMILY OF BIGFOOT

As a teenager growing up in the nineties, my friends and I were always on the lookout for new adventures to push the boundaries of our suburban existence. That summer, we stumbled upon an idea that would lead us to an encounter we could never forget. The day was hot and muggy when we decided to venture into the dense woods near our home for a camping trip. Little did we know that this journey would take a terrifying turn. The woods, known to us as "The Wild," were a labyrinth of towering trees and winding trails, a place where we could escape the confines of our everyday lives. We gathered our camping gear and loaded our backpacks with tents, sleeping bags, and a small stash of snacks. Armed with flashlights and a sense of invincibility, we set off. Our destination was a secluded spot by a tranquil stream. The journey was tough, but the anticipation of an unforgettable night kept us going. We set up our campsite, built a small fire, and settled in for the evening. The chatter of my friends and the crackling fire filled the air as night fell.

As darkness enveloped The Wild, a hush fell upon the forest. The only sounds were the occasional rustling of leaves and the distant call of an owl. We were miles away from civilization, and the sense of isolation was exhilarating. The first inkling that something was amiss came when the forest's nocturnal chorus fell silent. It was as if all the creatures of the night had suddenly vanished. My friends and I exchanged uneasy glances but brushed it off as just another peculiarity of the woods. Then, we heard it—a low, guttural growl that sent shivers down our spines. The firelight cast dancing shadows on the surrounding trees, and our imaginations began to run wild. We whispered to each other, trying to figure out the source of the sound. We contemplated raccoons, coyotes, or even a bear. We were all more than familiar with each and every animal that prowled and roamed around those woods because not only had we been taught from a very young age to recognize the sounds of predatory animals but also because we spent so much time out there that it was impossible for us not to notice which animals made which sounds. It was unlike anything any of us had ever heard before and since we all had grown up around those woods, that made it even scarier for us.

But as the growls grew louder and closer, we knew this was no ordinary forest creature. Panic began to grip us as we realized that whatever it was, it was enormous and definitely not an animal we could handle. Our flashlights trembled as we pointed them into the darkness, scanning the inky blackness for any sign of the intruder. And then, we saw it—a massive, hairy figure standing at the edge of our campsite. It was unlike anything we had ever seen. Towering at least eight feet tall, it had long, matted hair that hung from its body. Its eyes glowed with an unnatural, eerie light. The creature was unmistakably a Bigfoot. We were paralyzed with fear, unable to comprehend the enormity of the situation. We had all heard the legends about this creature before and most of us had grown up listening to either our parents or others in our families talking about it. Some of us were taught it was nothing more than a mere urban legend or a fantasy creature while the rest of us, me included, were taught that it was a supernatural being that really existed in various types of woodland areas all over the world. I was overwhelmed and somewhat in awe but the terror I was feeling would overshadow that at the time. All I wanted to do was get as far away from it as possible, though I admit a little part of my brain was excited by the prospect of telling my dad what we saw out there; of telling him I had come face to face with the elusive beast. The Bigfoot stared at us, its expression inscrutable, and then let out another bone-chilling growl. It took a step toward us, and that's when instinct kicked in. We scrambled to our feet, adrenaline coursing through our veins.

We grabbed our flashlights, and the blinding beams illuminated the creature's face. Its features were human-like but twisted in an unsettling way. The eyes, a deep, intelligent brown, held a strange mixture of curiosity and hostility. With trembling voices, we shouted and waved our lights, attempting to scare it away. But the Bigfoot seemed unimpressed by our feeble attempts. It took another step, causing the ground to shake beneath it. Fearful that it would approach even closer, we decided to make a strategic retreat. We moved slowly backward, maintaining eye contact with the creature. The woods, once familiar and welcoming, had transformed into a nightmarish labyrinth. It was then that we noticed something strange—the Bigfoot seemed to be protecting something behind it. Our fear gave way to curiosity, and we decided to investigate further. I know how stupid this sounds and I also know most people would have never stopped running for their lives but it was like we somehow knew it wasn't going to kill us. Granted we didn't know if it would hurt us or not but I guess that was a risk we were willing to take. I needed to know more about it because I knew my dad was going to flip out if I told him I just randomly crossed paths with a supernatural creature he had sworn was real, and that he had his own experience with when he was little, and I just ran from it. No, I had to investigate further. With great caution, we approached the creature once more, our lights still fixed on its face. We inched closer, and that's when we saw it—two smaller, juvenile Bigfoot crouched behind the massive figure. They were cowering, their eyes reflecting both fear and curiosity. The situation was surreal, and we didn't know what to make of it. We slowly realized that the Bigfoot family before us didn't seem intent on causing us harm; rather, they appeared to be protecting their young. The growls we had interpreted as aggression might have been a warning, a means of communicating their desire for us to leave. We conferred in whispers, deciding that it was best to heed the warning and leave the area. The Bigfoot family watched us closely as we retreated, and their eerie, glowing eyes followed our every move. We didn't dare look back until we had put a considerable distance between us and the creatures.

Back at our camp, we packed up our gear in record

time, our hands trembling with a mixture of fear and excitement. The woods, once a place of escape and adventure, had become a haunting realm of mystery and the unknown. As we made our way back through The Wild, we couldn't shake the feeling that we had just witnessed something extraordinary. The encounter with the Bigfoot family left us with more questions than answers. We wondered about the nature of these elusive creatures, their habits, and their interaction with humans. As we emerged from the woods and onto the outskirts of civilization, a sense of relief washed over us. We were exhausted, our clothes were tattered, and our faces bore the marks of fear and fatigue. We couldn't help but look back at the entrance to The Wild, wondering if the Bigfoot family was still lurking within. Reaching our homes was a surreal experience. As we entered the well-lit streets and comfortable houses, it was as if we had crossed a portal from a world of mystery and danger to one of safety and familiarity. We knew that our parents would be worried, and we faced the daunting task of explaining our wild adventure. I knew some of my friends were going to have a hard time getting their family to believe what we had all seen that day but I knew I would have no such issue. I was right and my father immediately wanted to go back out there and try to find the little family himself. My mother talked him out of it because she was concerned that if there were to be another encroachment on their territory right after my friends and I had seemingly done so, that it could push the creatures, especially the big one, over the edge and it would become extremely aggressive. He eventually listened to reason and has been searching in those woods ever since. He immediately started calling anyone and everyone he could think of and telling them all about what my friends and I had seen out there.

In the following weeks, we were interviewed by local news outlets and even met with experts who had studied Bigfoot sightings for years. Their questions delved into every detail of our encounter. They listened, nodded thoughtfully, and shared their own theories on what we had experienced. It was clear that our story was a rare and invaluable addition to the ongoing research about these elusive creatures. Over the years, we would recount our terrifying and astonishing encounter with friends and family, often met with skepticism and disbelief. But the memory of that night in the nineties remained etched in our minds. We had ventured into the wilderness seeking adventure, and we had found it in the most unexpected and surreal way. Our lives moved on, but the encounter with the Bigfoot family stayed with us. We read accounts of others who had experienced similar encounters with these mysterious creatures, and we began to appreciate the significance of our experience. It was a rare and unique insight into the world of Bigfoot, one that left us humbled and in awe of the mysteries that still linger in the remote corners of our planet. I've also become a part of the growing community of Bigfoot enthusiasts. I attended conferences, read books, and engaged in countless discussions about these elusive beings. The more I learned, the more I realized that our encounter was a rare and unique glimpse into a world that few would ever understand. I also discovered that researchers and enthusiasts were working diligently to collect evidence of Bigfoot's existence. They had captured blurry photographs, cast footprints, and recorded eerie vocalizations in the wilderness. While these findings were intriguing, they often left more questions than answers, fueling the ongoing debate about the existence of these creatures.

Today, as I recount the story of that unforgettable night in the nineties, I am left with a profound sense of wonder and respect for the natural world. The encounter with the Bigfoot family was a reminder that there are still secrets hidden within the depths of the wilderness, waiting for those adventurous enough to seek them out. And, while the memory of that night can still send shivers down my spine, it serves as a testament to the enduring mystery and wonder that our world has to offer. I continued to reflect on the night that had forever changed my perspective on the natural world. I remained grateful that no harm had come to my friends or me during our encounter with the Bigfoot family. It was a testament to the creatures' restraint and a reminder that, even in the face of the unknown, there could be a shared understanding between humans and the enigmatic beings that inhabit the remote corners of our planet. In the end, our encounter with the Bigfoot family left me with a profound sense of wonder and humility. It was a reminder that our world still held secrets waiting to be uncovered, mysteries that challenged our understanding of the natural world. The memory of that night in the nineties was a testament to the enduring sense of awe and fascination that our planet and its inhabitants can inspire. The encounter with the Bigfoot family had transformed me from a curious teenager into a lifelong explorer of the unknown. It was a story I would carry with me through the years, a reminder that even in our modern world, mysteries still lurk in the most unexpected places. The allure of the wild and the possibility of encountering the mysterious beings that call it home would forever drive my sense of adventure, and my fascination with the unexplained would never wane. As I look back on that life-altering experience, I can't help but wonder if the Bigfoot family we encountered still roams the remote woods, as elusive and enigmatic as ever. I remain captivated by the mysteries of The Wild and the creatures that call it home, and I continue to explore the world with a deep sense of respect for the unknown. The encounter with the Bigfoot family, though terrifying at the time, has become a treasured memory that reminds me of the wonders that can be found in the most unexpected places.

FIVE
A PROFOUND SECRET

I grew up in the midwestern part of the United States and I love it here just as much now as I always have. However, one night while I was doing something I did all the time, I had an experience that I still have trouble wrapping my head around and that sometimes feels more like it happened in a dream rather than in the woods I had grown so comfortable with. I decided to write about it here, now, because I recently came across some other encounter stories on the internet that seemed very similar to mine and I no longer feel so alone in my own mind or in my own experiences. Here's what happened: The Midwestern night was swathed in a deep, inky blackness, occasionally punctuated by the shimmering glow of stars. I was a curious teenager living in the heart of rural America, who had embarked on what turned out to be an extraordinary journey. My decision to take a shortcut through the dense woods to get back home after a visit to my friend's house was no big deal and as I already said it was something I had done all the time, without even thinking about it. This time though, it would turn out to be a decision that would haunt my dreams for years to come. As I trudged through the eerie, moonlit forest, my footsteps echoed through the silence of the night. There was nothing about being alone in the woods that ever really scared me or made me uncomfortable and by that time it was like second nature to me. I had come to enjoy the walks as they were some of very few times I was able to have some peace and quiet by myself. I was one of seven kids in a small house with both parents. So, yeah, normally I loved my walks in the dark, but on that night, right from the very beginning of my walk, something felt different. It was an unusually warm evening for the Midwest, with a soft breeze rustling the leaves and a hint of rain in the air. The distant sound of crickets and the occasional hoot of an owl were my only companions.

My unease began when I noticed a sudden, brilliant flash in the sky. It was unlike any meteor or shooting star I'd ever seen. The light was an otherworldly, vivid blue that illuminated the entire forest for a brief moment before vanishing into the void. I froze in my tracks, heart pounding in my chest, and gazed up at the sky, my breath catching in my throat. What had just happened? The strange occurrence was enough to make me contemplate turning back, to retrace my steps and forget this shortcut through the woods. That had never happened before and I remember stopping for several moments in order to contemplate what to do next. But there was something within me, a reckless curiosity that was a hallmark of my teenage years, that drove me forward. Against my better judgment, I decided to investigate the source of the eerie light. The woods grew darker and denser as I ventured deeper into the heart of the forest. The only thing that kept me going was the distant, tantalizing glow, a beacon in the dark, guiding me onward. My imagination ran wild, conjuring images of extraterrestrial encounters and government experiments. The very thought sent shivers down my spine. You see, I was one of those kids that really enjoyed playing fantasy role playing games. I also loved science fiction movies, television shows and even comic books. I voraciously devoured anything and everything I could get my hands on about extraterrestrials but I never thought of them as anything other than fiction. It made perfect sense though that they were what I immediately thought of when I first saw that light and even more so as I advanced towards it.

The air grew heavy with a sense of foreboding as I neared the light's origin. The underbrush crackled beneath

my feet, and the trees seemed to close in around me. It felt
as though the woods themselves were conspiring to keep
me away. But I pressed on, curiosity outweighing my fear.
Finally, I reached a small clearing, and there it was: the
source of the strange light. Hovering just a few feet above
the ground was a saucer-like craft, its surface adorned with
intricate patterns that seemed to shift and change. The
vessel was cloaked in an ethereal glow, its edges diffusing
into the surrounding darkness. It was like nothing I had
ever seen before, a testament to technology far beyond our
comprehension. It reminded me of a craft I had seen on
one of my favorite television shows. I had to keep blinking
in order to convince myself this was all really happening to
me. There was a mixture of terror, curiosity and excitement that overwhelmed me. As I stared in awe at the
mysterious craft, I became aware of movement beneath it.
My heart leaped into my throat as I saw them – the creatures. They were unlike any beings I had ever encountered,
and they emanated an aura of dread that sent a shiver
down my spine. Their skin was a sickly shade of green,
stretched taut over bony, elongated bodies. Their limbs
were spindly, ending in claw-like appendages that
scratched the ground. Their heads were disproportionately
large, with bulging, lidless eyes that glowed with an eerie,
phosphorescent light. These beings were the stuff of nightmares, the embodiment of terror.

A sense of primal fear gripped me, and my instinct was to flee, to run as far from this bizarre encounter as possible. But I was frozen in place, my feet rooted to the ground, as though I had become invisible to the world around me. I watched in helpless horror as the creatures moved about, oblivious to my presence. They seemed to be examining the flora and fauna of the forest, taking samples, and making strange, guttural noises. It was as if they were conducting a survey, cataloging the life of this rural Midwestern woodland. The light from the craft above cast long, eerie shadows that danced on the forest floor, adding to the surreal ambiance of the scene. There was a part of me that wanted to approach them but the dread and terror just looking at them instilled in me kept me from doing so. I often wonder what would have happened should they have found me or knew that I was there. What if they did know and were just pretending as though they didn't? While these thoughts are easy for me to ruminate over now, in hindsight, there was something inside of me that knew it would be the death of me or worse to let my presence be known. I knew deep down that if they had known I was there they would have either attacked me, taken me or something much worse would have happened. Sometimes, in my nightmares, they've abducted me and the more I see about abductions on the news, in television shows and on the internet, I often wonder if this was all part of the same experience, with the nightmares being just a screen memory of something that really happened. I know I am getting off track but that's what happens whenever I go over the events of that night in depth and with great detail; I become very confused and start thinking ahead of myself. Okay let me get back to the woods.

For what felt like an eternity, I remained hidden in the shadows, observing the alien beings as they went about their business. The dread that had initially enveloped me was gradually replaced by a strange mix of curiosity and fascination. I couldn't deny the overwhelming desire to understand what I was witnessing, to bridge the gap between our worlds. The atmosphere around the creatures seemed charged with an inexplicable energy, an unspoken connection to the cosmos. I could almost feel the weight of their otherworldly knowledge, and it left me in awe. As the minutes stretched on, my fear began to wane, replaced by a sense of wonder. I couldn't help but wonder what had brought these beings to our remote corner of the world. Were they explorers from a distant galaxy, curious about life on Earth? Or were they something more sinister, conducting experiments on our planet? That just didn't seem right to me though and I felt like they were evil, somehow, or at least how us human beings see evil as being. I felt like something outside of me was summoning me, trying to get me to inch closer for a better look. It was like some sort of unseen force was trying to make me start moving closer so as to expose my presence to the horrible looking beings. However, just as suddenly as that pull started to take hold of me, it stopped and the alien beings abruptly stopped their activities. Their heads turned skyward, and a series of guttural, clicking sounds emanated from them. The craft above began to shimmer, its cloaking field fluctuating before gradually fading away to reveal its true form.

The saucer-like vessel was a marvel of technology, a fusion of sleek, metallic surfaces and intricate, pulsating lights. It hung suspended in the air for a moment before shooting upward with a breathtaking speed, disappearing into the vastness of the night sky. The creatures, too, vanished into thin air, leaving no trace of their presence. I was left standing alone in the clearing, my heart pounding, my mind reeling. Had it all been a hallucination, a figment of my overactive imagination? Nowadays I know for absolute fact that it really happened but as it was happening I was so amazed. confused. I often wonder too if my mind was purposely muddled. The forest had returned to its natural state, the silence broken only by the distant sounds of wildlife. As I began to make my way back through the woods, I couldn't shake the feeling that I had glimpsed something truly extraordinary. The memory of those alien beings, their craft, and the strange light in the sky would stay with me for the rest of my life, a secret I could never fully share or explain to anyone. Upon finally returning home, I grappled with the overwhelming urge to tell someone about my bizarre encounter, but I knew that no one would believe me. After all, who would believe the story of a teenager from rural Midwestern America who claimed to have witnessed an extraterrestrial event in the heart of the woods? Back in the 1980s when all of this happened to me, it was unheard of to discuss such things as if they were real, let alone to confess to having experienced something like that yourself. I had to keep it a secret and it tore me up inside. There were times I wanted to just blurt out what happened to me but I had to consider the times I was living in. Not too many people, if anyone, would've believed me. Heck, I couldn't even convince myself at times, questioning whether it had all been a vivid dream or a trick of the mind. But the sense of dread and wonder, the memory of those terrifying alien beings and their otherworldly craft, were all too real to dismiss.

Decades have passed since that fateful night, and life in our quiet corner of rural America has gone on as it always has. I've grown into adulthood, built a career, and started a family of my own. Yet, I can't help but feel that I carry a profound secret, a knowledge of something beyond the ordinary that few will ever understand. I've revisited the woods countless times, searching for any trace of the strange encounter, but the clearing where it all happened remains unchanged, as if frozen in time. The feeling of being watched persists, and I can't escape the sense that I'm being monitored by eyes not of this world. One thing is certain: the night I followed that strange light into the woods, I stepped into a realm of the unknown, a world where our reality intersected with something far more profound and mysterious. And though the fear still lingers, so does the unquenchable curiosity, the desire to understand the uncharted depths of our universe. The encounter in the woods that night was a revelation, a glimpse into a realm that defied explanation, and it's a story that will forever define my existence. I live on, unharmed physically, but forever changed by the inexplicable, by the terror and wonder of the unknown.

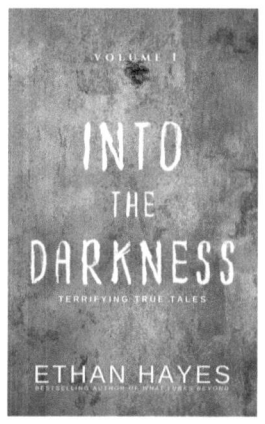

HORRIFYING FACELESS CREATURE

I grew up in Arkansas and I lived basically in the middle of the woods. I don't mean to sound cliche because I read a lot of these encounter stories because I am always searching for answers to what I saw and I know that most of them start like that. It's true though and I think that has a lot to do with why I saw what I did. I feel like the forests and woods of the world are places where there are lines between realms and dimensions and sometimes things cross from one to another, whether on purpose or accidentally. Most of the time I don't think anyone notices but I believe that when human beings end up coming across something like what I saw, something unexplainable, that's one of the reasons why. We simply see something we shouldn't have and are then left to live the rest of our lives with that information and most of the time we have no idea what to even do with it all. I was seven years old and was camping in some woods by my house with my mom, dad and older sister. We went camping several times a year, usually with the change of the seasons and it never got boring or old for us. It was the nineteen sixties and there wasn't a lot to do otherwise. Not if you didn't have a lot of money anyway and my family definitely fit under that category. Now, I want to say right here and now that, as strange as it may sound, this was only the first of four times I saw something similar to what I'm about to describe to you. It came in a different guise every time and while this encounter was with "a little girl" it wasn't always that way. It did always happen in the same place though, this one patch of dense woods about a mile away from my grandparent's house. They lived a twenty minute drive from me and my parents and we visited with them a lot. I don't pretend to know what it all means but I wonder if I was chosen or, like I just said, if I just happened to be in the wrong place at the wrong time.

We left my grandparents house in the middle of the day. We had our campervan all packed up and ready to go. We didn't camp in tents anymore because my mom said my sister and I always had a really hard time when we would have to do it that way. I guess we didn't like lying in the dirt or whatever but she never really elaborated and simply said it made her job easier. We were familiar with the woods and spent a lot of time in the ones surrounding our house too. It was scary at night, I remember always feeling like something or someone was watching us. It was the first year we were using the campervan and my sister and I were very excited. We thought it was really fancy and didn't even want to leave it once we parked it in our campsite. My dad was an avid outdoorsman and wanted my sister and I to learn how to survive out there but I think he was giving in to my mom with the rental van. The first night there passed fairly normal and we were all in bed by eleven that night. The next day my mom asked my sister and I if we wanted to go and pick some berries with her. I eagerly said that I did but my sister had already agreed to go fishing with my dad. My mom grabbed some larger bushel baskets and we headed out on our way. We all agreed to meet back at the van in four hours in order to have lunch. Mom gave me my basket and told me not to stray too far away from her. I always wandered off as a kid. I liked to explore and while my parents encouraged that, my mother liked to always have her eyes on me. We picked berries for about an hour and suddenly I was really tired. My mom told me to sit on a large rock and stay with the bushels we had already almost filled while she went and just finished collecting enough berries to fill her last basket. I agreed to stay there and off she went.

My mom still swears she had only been gone ten minutes but in my memory she had been gone for so long I started to get really worried. I yelled out for her but she didn't answer me and so I screamed out to her but still received no answer. I had just started crying when I heard a noise coming from behind me. I heard giggling and turned around just in time to see a little girl in a white dress running away from me. I could only see her back but she had been wearing an old fashioned dress, even for the time it was then, and she had long, dark brown pigtails in her hair. They were braided. I ran after her and she continued to giggle and run deeper into the woods. The fact that I had told my mother I wouldn't move didn't even cross my mind. I was only seven years old and thought that I had found a new playmate. It didn't occur to my young brain that there shouldn't have been another unsupervised child out there, especially not one who was wearing a dress and who had such seemingly perfect hair. I yelled out to the little girl but she didn't turn around and after I chased her for almost five whole minutes, she turned a bend and seemed to have disappeared. I was confused but even worse than that I realized I had gotten lost while chasing her. I stood still and looked all around me but the woods looked a little different. How they looked different I couldn't quite put my finger on but the colors almost seemed brighter while the previously bright and sunny sky had gotten very dark. There were gray clouds in the sky and this only elevated my fear and confusion. I called out for my mother but again received no answer so I yelled for the little girl to come out. I had become convinced she was hiding from me. Just as I turned and started to walk the other way, I heard her giggling again. It was coming from behind one of the trees nearby. I ran over there and saw the same girl, on her knees and facing the tree. Her hands looked like they were in a praying position. I tapped her on the shoulder but she didn't even seem to know I was there. She didn't acknowledge me.

I was very annoyed and mad at the time because she had gotten me lost and then she was ignoring me. I grabbed her shoulder to try and get her to turn around and face me but it was the worst mistake of my life. She did turn around then but when she did I saw that she had no face. It wasn't like there were holes where her eyes and nose should've been but it just looked like nothing. Someone else who has encountered this same type of terrifying entity described it as looking like someone stretched a piece of fabric over a football. It was terrifying and I stumbled backwards and screamed. I was on my behind then and the little girl suddenly stood up. She was about five feet tall, so taller than I was, and she had white skin. Her arms were extremely long and her hands, while otherwise looking normal, hung down to her ankles. She took two steps towards me and stopped again as I tried to scoot back on my behind to get away from her. I didn't have enough room to stand up yet and also, my legs were far too shaky to even try to get up and get away. Then, as I screamed, the little girl turned her head to one side as though she were just staring at me and was very confused. All of this would have been enough but it got worse. She then started to mumble, as though she were trying to talk but her mouth was covered. It wasn't that it was covered so much that it wasn't there and I didn't know what to do. Finally, I couldn't take anymore and I got up to run. I heard the girl mumbling louder and incessantly as she followed behind me. She never ran but she walked very fast. It started to rain and I started to cry. I turned around to see if she was still chasing me and she was. I turned back around to watch where I was going so I didn't fall again and I slammed right into my father. He and my sister were making their way back from fishing. I screamed and fought with my dad to let me go before I realized who he was. He grabbed me and asked me what in the world I was doing. I snapped out of it.

I immediately looked behind me again but there was no one there. She had just been there a second ago and I realized too that it wasn't raining anymore. Not only that, I wasn't wet at all and it was almost as though it had never rained in the first place. I frantically tried to tell my dad and sister what had just happened to me. My sister thought I was just trying to scare her but my father looked more concerned than anything else. He asked me where my mother was and I told him I didn't know. We went back to the camp but my mom wasn't there either and we were in the middle of trying to figure out where we should go to try and find her when she came running through the woods. The minute she saw all of us she looked instantly relieved and ran over to me. She had tears in her eyes and it was like she couldn't believe what she was seeing. I tried once again to tell everyone what happened but none of them believed me. It turned out I had traveled nearly two miles from where we were berry picking to the area where my sister and father had been fishing. I had done that in a matter of mere minutes. Four and a half hours had passed which means I lost about two hours of time that I still have no memory of to this very day. My mom said she never went and didn't hear me far enough that she wouldn't have been able to hear me calling her at all. I got in a lot of trouble and wasn't allowed to participate in any of the fun activities with my dad and sister the whole next day. I had to stay in the campervan with my mom because they thought I had simply not listened to them and wandered off. However, none of them could explain how I had gotten so far in such a short amount of time, but I really don't think that they wanted to. It was all too much for them to handle.

I often wonder if I was abducted or something that day. The other three times I saw a similar faceless entity I also lost time, have no memory of what happened during the missing time and I had always seemed to travel much further than I should have been able to when looking for whatever image the entity presented itself as. I say that because I certainly don't believe I was dealing with an actual little girl, for obvious reasons. I think whatever lurked underneath the guise was pure evil and acted as some sort of lure. Whatever the reason and whomever the entities are, it all felt extremely nefarious to me from the moment I realized I was lost that first time. I don't talk about this in my private life or publicly and aside from trying to tell my parents and my sister that one time on the first day that it all happened, no one knows what happened to me. The other encounters happened throughout different times in my life. The second time I was a teenager and the other two times I was an adult already. It makes no rational sense, I know that, but there isn't anything to explain any of it otherwise either. It was terrifying and the implications of the distances traveled in such a short time in woodland areas I am usually very familiar with in general and the missing time are absolutely horrifying. I don't know if I was chosen or if I randomly stumbled upon the phenomenon and the powers that be, the ones who make these encounters possible and maybe even the ones behind the faceless entities, decided I was a good candidate for further experiences with them. It's all very confusing, I know, but that's really all there is to this particular encounter.

———

INTO THE DARKNESS

Publisher's Excerpt 2
LEGENDS AND STORIES: FROM THE PACIFIC CREST TRAIL

WHITE EYED KID

Nestled along the Santa Lucia Mountains in California's Big Sur region, there exists a mystery as ancient as the native tribes that first populated the area. Silhouetted against the twilight sky, figures known as the "Dark Watchers" have been reported by observers for centuries. These elusive, shadowy figures, often spotted at great distances along the ridges and peaks, have become the stuff of local legend and folklore.

Origins:

The origins of the Dark Watchers remain shrouded in mystery. Local Native American tribes, such as the Chumash, have stories and legends that date back over a millennium, some of which make reference to shadowy figures or entities in the mountains. Yet, it's difficult to ascertain whether these tales directly relate to the contemporary Dark Watcher legends or represent different cultural narratives altogether.

Before European settlers arrived in the region, the area was inhabited by the Chumash people for thousands of years. Their rich tapestry of oral tradition and legends provides some potential early references to the Dark Watchers. The Chumash painted intricate cave and rock art, which some believe could depict the enigmatic figures. While direct evidence connecting the Chumash legends to the Dark Watchers is scant, the stories of "nunashish" or otherworldly beings from their folklore might have some parallels.

The Chumash believed in a variety of spiritual entities,

both benevolent and malevolent. The mountains and wilderness areas were considered sacred, liminal spaces where the veil between the physical and spiritual world was thin. Entities dwelling in these regions were believed to hold significant power and knowledge.

The phenomenon of the Dark Watchers wasn't restricted to indigenous tales. Early Spanish settlers and explorers in California also had stories of "Los Vigilantes Oscuros" or "The Old Ones" (sometimes referred to as "Los Antiguos"). These figures were said to appear at the end of the day, standing silently and looking out into the distance. Much like later tales, they would vanish the moment someone tried to approach them or looked away.

It's worth noting that the Spanish settlers had no known direct contact with the Chumash in terms of shared legends. This separation makes the similarity in stories even more intriguing and gives credence to the idea that something genuinely unexplained might have been occurring in the mountains.

Over time, with the influx of more settlers, miners during the gold rush, and eventually modern Californians, the stories of the Dark Watchers evolved and merged. Each generation, each group brought its own interpretation and experiences to the legend, enriching it.

As is often the case with folklore, pinpointing a single "origin" is challenging. Stories evolve, intermingle, and change over time based on cultural, environmental, and societal factors. The Dark Watchers legend, with its ancient roots and continued modern sightings, exemplifies this dynamic nature of folklore.

In essence, while the origins of the Dark Watchers remain elusive, their enduring presence in the tales of various cultures and eras speaks to their deep-rooted significance in the region's collective consciousness.

Descriptions:

Witnesses often describe the Dark Watchers as tall, sometimes over ten feet, humanoid figures that stand motionless, gazing out over the valleys and sea. They appear around dusk or dawn, and they always stand in silhouette, making their specific features difficult to discern. Some accounts attribute them with flowing cloaks or wide-brimmed hats, but these details vary.

- **Physical Stature**

- **Height**: They are frequently described as tall, imposing figures. The height often ranges from being slightly taller than the average human to descriptions of them being giants, standing over 10 feet tall.
- **Silhouette**: The most consistent aspect of the Dark Watchers is their shadowy appearance.

They're nearly always described as dark, featureless silhouettes. This makes discerning specific features difficult, and they usually appear this way regardless of the angle of light, which adds to their enigmatic nature.

-Clothing and Attire

- **Cloaks**: One of the most frequently noted details is that these figures often appear to be wearing long, flowing cloaks or robes that billow gently, even when there's no wind.
- **Hats**: In several accounts, the Dark Watchers are described as wearing wide-brimmed hats, reminiscent of styles that might have been common among Spanish settlers or even earlier periods.
- **Staffs or Walking Sticks**: Some witnesses have reported seeing the figures holding staffs or walking sticks, further adding to their mysterious traveler or watcher persona.

- Behavior and Demeanor

- **Stillness**: The Dark Watchers are not usually described as actively doing much. They stand still, often in places that would be challenging for a human to reach, such as a steep ridge or mountaintop.

- **Observing**: True to their name, they are often just watching or gazing out into the distance. Their focus could be the horizon, the valleys below, or sometimes, according to unnerved witnesses, the people who spot them.
- **Vanishing Act**: One of the most consistently eerie attributes is their ability to disappear. They don't typically walk away or move out of sight. Witnesses often describe turning away for a moment or momentarily losing sight of the figure due to an obstacle, and then the Dark Watcher is gone when they look back.
- **Lack of Interaction**: There are rarely, if ever, accounts of the Dark Watchers interacting with those who see them. They don't communicate or acknowledge witnesses; they just observe.

In sum, the Dark Watchers are characterized by their passive, observing nature and their consistent, shadowy appearance. The occasional details of old-world clothing or accessories add to the timeless, eerie quality of the legend. Given the range of descriptions over the years and the inherent mystery surrounding them, they've become an enigmatic staple in the folklore of the region.

Literary References:
- John Steinbeck's *Flight*

- **Reference**: In his short story *Flight*, John Steinbeck briefly alludes to the Dark Watchers. Steinbeck, who was deeply familiar with the landscapes and lore of California, writes:

    "Pepe looked up to the top of the next dry withered ridge. He saw a dark form against the sky, a man's figure standing on top of a rock, and he glanced away quickly not to appear curious."

- **Context**: *Flight* tells the story of Pepe, a young man who becomes an inadvertent outlaw and then a fugitive, journeying into the wild terrains of the region. As Pepe travels through the landscape, the brief encounter with the Dark Watcher mirrors the sense of foreboding and the vast unknown that the protagonist confronts.

-Robinson Jeffers and *Such Counsels You Gave To Me*

- **Reference**: Robinson Jeffers, a prominent American poet who lived for much of his life in Big Sur, California, also touches upon the Dark Watchers in his poem *Such Counsels You Gave To Me*. The stanza reads:

  "He thought it might be one of the watchers,Who are often seen in this length of coast-range,Forms that look human to human eyes,But are certainly not human. They come from behind ridges to watch."

- **Context**: Jeffers was renowned for his deep connection to the rugged landscapes of the Californian coast and frequently intertwined the natural and the mystical in his works. In this poem, the mention of the Watchers, those almost-human entities that come forth to observe, evokes a sense of the sublime—a mix of awe and fear in the face of vast, mysterious nature.

-Literary Impact and Analysis

Both Steinbeck and Jeffers had an intimate knowledge of the California landscape and its associated lore. Their allusions to the Dark Watchers not only acknowledge the legends but also harness the eerie, mysterious essence of these figures to underscore themes of insignificance, the unknown, and man's relationship with nature.

The use of these figures in literature serves to elevate them from mere local myths to symbols that can be employed to evoke specific emotions and themes. When read in the context of their larger works, the Dark Watchers serve as more than just legends; they represent the vast, unknowable mysteries that surround us, the age-old tales rooted in a place, and the eerie feeling of being watched when one thinks they are alone.

It's also noteworthy that literature can amplify local legends, and in the case of the Dark Watchers, mentions by such prominent writers might have helped perpetuate and spread their lore to a wider audience, further embedding them in the collective consciousness.

Theories:

Several theories attempt to explain the phenomenon of the Dark Watchers, though none provide a comprehensive answer:

- **Optical Illusions**: Some believe that the watchers are merely optical illusions. The interplay of light during the twilight hours can create elongated shadows, and the human brain, known for its pattern-recognition tendencies, might interpret these shadows as humanoid figures.
- **Hallucinations**: Factors like fatigue, isolation, and the play of light can sometimes induce hallucinations. Individuals trekking or living in the mountains, under certain conditions, might perceive things that aren't really there.
- **Spiritual Entities**: For those inclined towards the supernatural or metaphysical, the Dark Watchers are sometimes seen as ancient spirits or protectors of the land, watching over the valleys and inhabitants below.
- **Unrecorded History**: Some speculate that these figures might be linked to an unrecorded or forgotten history of the region, where real watchers or guardians once stood sentinel and over time became part of local myth.

Modern Sightings

The allure of the Dark Watchers is intensified by sporadic reports of sightings in recent times. These contemporary accounts often come from hikers, travelers, and locals who are familiar with the landscape yet are left puzzled and unnerved by their experiences. Here's an account from a modern sighting:

A Hiker's Tale

Jenna, an avid hiker from San Luis Obispo, shared her experience from a late afternoon trek in 2015. She was hiking a less-traveled path in the Santa Lucia Mountains, enjoying the solitude and the play of golden light as the sun began its descent.

As she made her way along a ridge, Jenna noticed a figure standing atop a distant peak. Thinking it was another hiker, she continued her trek but couldn't shake off the feeling that something was odd about the lone figure. Its stillness was unsettling. There was no visible movement, no adjusting of a backpack, no taking in the view with hands on hips. Just a stationary, dark silhouette against the backdrop of the setting sun.

Curiosity piqued, Jenna decided to take out her binoculars. Through the enhanced view, the figure appeared even more perplexing. It was undoubtedly humanoid, tall, and draped in what seemed like a flowing garment, perhaps a cloak.

There were no discernible facial features—just a shadowy, blank face.

Feeling a mix of excitement and apprehension, she decided to make her way towards the figure, thinking perhaps she'd find a fellow hiker with an interesting tale of why they were standing so still for so long. But as she neared the spot, traversing a dip in the terrain which momentarily obstructed her view, the figure vanished. No trace, no footprints, nothing.

Jenna knew the legends of the Dark Watchers, but she had always relegated them to the realm of folklore. However, her personal encounter left her questioning. She hadn't felt threatened, but the encounter had an uncanny quality that stayed with her. When she shared her experience with fellow hikers and locals, she found that she wasn't alone. Others too had their tales, their brief sightings of the shadowy watchers of the Santa Lucia Mountains.

Modern reports like Jenna's are intriguing because they come from individuals who often have no prior inclination to believe in local myths or legends. They're typically rational, grounded in their understanding of the world, yet their experiences challenge their own skepticism.

While no concrete evidence, like photographs or videos, has emerged to substantiate these modern sightings, they continue to be a topic of intrigue and discussion in local communities and among those who trek the trails of the Santa Lucia Mountains. These encounters add a contemporary layer to the age-old tales, ensuring that the legend of the Dark Watchers endures in the modern psyche.

Conclusion

The Dark Watchers of the Santa Lucia Mountains represent one of those enduring mysteries where myth, history, and natural phenomena intersect. They are a testament to the human spirit's desire to understand, interpret, and at times, marvel at the unknown. Whether they are mere shadows, optical illusions, or something more profound, the Dark Watchers continue to inspire wonder and curiosity in all who hear their story.

———

LEGENDS AND STORIES: FROM THE PACIFIC CREST TRAIL

SIX

BLACKTHORN GROVE

In the heart of England, nestled within the dense and ancient woodlands, there exists a place shrouded in myth and mystery. This remote and isolated corner of the countryside, known to a few as Blackthorn Grove, was my chosen destination for a camping trip, seeking solace and respite from the modern world. I had visited this place a few times but I hadn't been back there since I was a little girl and would go camping or hiking there with my family. I remember being enchanted with Blackthorn Grove in a way that I had never been with any other place we ever spent time and that's saying a great deal because camping and spending time in the great outdoors was something we all did as a family several times a year my whole life. I randomly thought about it when I was finally

able to take some time to go camping myself and I had
wondered why we just seemingly stopped going there for
no apparent reason when I was around twelve years old. I
tried to think if there was anything specific that had
happened that we never went back there but I couldn't
remember anything. I didn't want to be going somewhere
and getting myself into something dangerous and asked
my father if there was a reason we had stopped going there
but continued to go to all of our other favorite spots and if
he knew of any reason why I should maybe go somewhere
else as well. My dad told me there was no reason but then
he pretended like he hadn't realized we stopped going
there and that it was something that had happened inad-
vertently. That was suspicious but I decided not to press
him and knew that if there were any specific dangers that
he knew about in Blackthorn Grove he would have immediately told me. I was excited and couldn't wait to get
there. It had always seemed to me like an enchanted forest
like the ones from my favorite fairytales and I felt like a
little girl again as I planned the trip. Little did I know that
this tranquil haven held secrets and legends that would
defy belief. The journey to Blackthorn Grove was a
journey back in time.

The road leading to this secluded wilderness wound
through picturesque villages, where stone cottages with
thatched roofs stood in quiet reverence of centuries past.

As I ventured deeper into the countryside, the rolling hills and endless meadows gave way to dense, ancient woodlands, untouched by the march of time. As I arrived at the edge of Blackthorn Grove, I felt a distinct change in the atmosphere. The air grew still, and the trees stood tall and imposing, their branches intertwining to form an almost impenetrable canopy. The forest floor was a labyrinth of ferns and moss, and the rich scent of damp earth hung in the air. It was here that I chose to set up camp, a small clearing illuminated by the dappled sunlight that managed to filter through the dense foliage. My tent was pitched amidst the towering trees, and a crackling campfire brought a sense of warmth to the otherwise foreboding surroundings. The day passed slowly, as I explored the woods, marveled at the vibrant birdlife, and listened to the whispers of the wind through the leaves. It was just as I had remembered and hadn't lost any of its enchantment. I was delighted. I will admit there was an almost overwhelming sense of sadness that seemed to almost permeate the air but I had always been sensitive to the energy around me, though it isn't something I can really explain, and I just assumed that it was maybe something residual from something that had happened there at some point in time that had left an indelible mark on the forest itself. Things like that happen from time to time and eventually it faded away. The deeper I traversed the woods, the more alive with primal energy the forest became and it was something else I was very aware of as well. It was as if it had existed in this timeless state since the dawn of time. I think that's why I had let the overwhelming sadness go, because with the deeper I traveled into the woods it had sort of faded away and where I set up my camp the air was more electrifying than anything else. As night fell, I retreated to my campfire, its flickering light casting eerie, dancing shadows on the trees that surrounded me. The sounds of the night began to emerge—the distant hoot of an owl, the rustling of unseen creatures in the underbrush, and the gentle trickling of a nearby stream. The solitude was both peaceful and unnerving, a reminder of how truly remote I was.

It was during the deep, velvet darkness of night that my encounter occurred. As I lay in my tent, the haunting melody of what sounded like a lone flute permeated the air and all of the atmosphere around me. Within minutes the flute grew louder, pulling me further into the depths of an uncanny, isolated world. My heart raced, and beads of sweat formed on my forehead. I was instantly scared and also I became very aware, almost immediately, how vulnerable I was out there at night all by myself. After all, it was one of the first times I had ever been out there where there were no other people out there camping at all, whether with me or separately. With bated breath, I unzipped my tent and peered into the inky blackness. A surreal glow beckoned from deep within the woods, and a sense of impending doom washed over me. Something was lurking in the shadows, something both ancient and unnatural. I reached for my flashlight because I intended on shining it into the woods but I couldn't immediately find it and I refused to take my eyes off of the glow itself. I finally gave up on finding the flashlight and just sat there peering out into the darkness. I had always had a very active imagination and all sorts of strange and terrifying things, with extraterrestrials being among them, all running through my mind in those few seconds. I didn't know what to do and so I just waited. It would only take a moment more to see what I was dealing with.

The creature emerged with an ethereal grace, like a phantom gliding through the trees. It was part of the forest, an embodiment of the wild, and it cast an eerie spell upon the night. The creature's eyes, large and sorrowful, bore into mine with an unspoken message—an invitation to a world beyond human comprehension. As it drew closer, I noticed the intricate patterns etched into its fur. Each line, each curve, told a story of countless seasons, whispered secrets passed down through the ages. The antlers atop its head resembled gnarled branches, adorned with luminous mushrooms that emitted an otherworldly glow, casting an eerie pallor on its surroundings. It walked on its hind legs but the top part of it, from the stomach on up, was human. It had a perfectly chiseled chest and abdomen and it looked more physically fit than it seemed possible a human being could get. Not even if they spent countless hours at the gym every single day of the week for years did it seem likely a human man or woman would ever get their body to look like this thing. It had a beautiful face, also looking like it was chiseled from stone into a god that then started moving around and was coming right towards me. I felt the creature's presence, even before I laid eyes on it. I felt its energy, as it approached, its human looking fingers extending towards me. A chilling sensation swept over me as its touch unlocked memories buried deep within the forest's heart. I saw the changing of seasons, the flow of centuries, and the enduring spirit of the woods. In the creature's gaze, I glimpsed the sorrow of a thousand years, the weight of centuries of solitude and guardianship. It was a sentinel, a guardian of Blackthorn Grove, an embodiment of the forest's wisdom. I don't know how I knew it was a sentinel, it just reminded me of something I had seen at some point in my childhood in one of the fairy-tales I liked to read. It was unnatural, but yet it was perfectly natural. I know that doesn't make much sense but sometimes the words just aren't there to describe everything I saw and sensed that night accurately.

With a gentle, haunting flute melody, the creature withdrew, leaving me with a sense of reverence and profound understanding. Keep in mind it wasn't the creature that was playing the flute and I honestly don't know where the melody was coming from but it seemed like it might have just been coming from the forest itself. The forest sighed as if it, too, had shared in our strange communion. I sat there in complete disbelief for a long while. I wanted to follow the creature but something inside of me told me that it had gone to another realm, one where I wouldn't have been allowed to enter, even if I ever had been able to find it, which was unlikely. I wondered and thought about so many things in those moments, including if my father or someone else in my family had experienced something similar and if that was the reason why we never went back there and it was never even really discussed again. I debated on whether or not I should tell anyone and decided against it. It was like I had been made privy to some sort of eternal and immortal secret and I felt like I had been entrusted with it and therefore chose to keep it to myself. This is the first time I am discussing it and as you know I am doing so anonymously, and that's for the very reasons I just listed here for you. As dawn approached, I prepared to leave Blackthorn Grove, forever changed by my encounter. The woods had granted me a glimpse into the enigmatic heart of nature, leaving me both haunted and enlightened. My reverence for the untamed places of the world had deepened, and I left with a deep respect for the mysteries that endure within the wild. The journey back through the rolling hills and ancient villages was uneventful, but the memories of Blackthorn Grove would stay with me forever. In the quiet of the forest and the mournful tune of the half-deer, half-man creature, I had found a connection to a world beyond the human realm. As I returned to the modern world, I knew that I had been granted a rare and haunting gift—the knowledge that the ancient guardians of the woods still watched over their domains, their presence a reminder of the enduring mysteries of the natural world. The encounter with the half-deer, half-man creature had changed me in ways I couldn't fully grasp. It was a testament to the enigmatic forces that reside in the heart of nature, and I carried its haunting memory with me, a constant reminder of the mysteries that lie just beyond the edge of our understanding. Thank you for giving me the space to be able to tell my story and I hope everyone who reads it can do so while withholding judgment of what I experienced. I didn't do drugs or drink and I definitely wasn't sleeping. It wasn't a dream, though sometimes it feels like it might have been. I am currently planning a trip back there, by myself, to see what other secrets of the forest

I can uncover, but I'm really going back because I feel like it's calling me there. Be it the sentinel or something else altogether, I don't feel like I can deny the allure of the calling any longer than I already have. If I come across anything else, I will surely write about it.

SEVEN
BENDING REALITY

The year was 1979, and I found myself in a familiar area near my house, nestled within the woods that surrounded a serene lake. It had always been a place of solace, a refuge from the demands of everyday life. My bond with mother nature while in those woods was always so strong, as I had camped by the lake and swum in its waters countless times. But on this particular night, something eerie and unsettling would shatter the tranquility I had come to cherish. I had always been drawn to the mysteries of the night, the secrets that it concealed under its cloak of darkness. I watched more than my fair share of horror movies and I was always looking around the corner or over my shoulder for the boogeyman but in a fun way. I am still like that today, loving scary movies and becoming excited by a good jump scare. I just found comfort in the darkness of the night I guess. The moon hung high in the sky, casting a silvery glow on the calm waters of the lake. The night was warm, inviting, and it beckoned me to venture beyond the confines of my tent. As I stepped out into the moonlit night, the eerie glow of something strange caught my eye. It was a pulsating, unearthly light that pierced through the darkness of the woods. It beckoned me like a siren's call, and I stumbled towards it, my steps uncertain and heavy. The light cast strange, shifting patterns on the trees, like some kind of supernatural aurora. As I drew closer to the source of the light, I felt a strange sensation wash over me. It was as though reality itself was warping and bending, like a dream that had become all too real. The air crackled with energy, and my skin prickled as I passed through the source of the light. There was barely enough time for me to be scared, but nonetheless the second I walked into that twisting and shifting light, I regretted it, and I knew I had made a fatal mistake. Another thought went through my head in that moment too and that was that things like this don't happen to people in real life!

I emerged on the other side in a place that defied all logic and reason. The forest had transformed into an otherworldly landscape, a realm of shadows and strange, twisted forms. Unearthly beings lurked in the darkness, their features indistinct and nightmarish. The creatures moved with an unnatural grace, their movements a grotesque parody of life. They had elongated limbs, jagged, angular features, and eyes that glowed with an unholy light. As they slithered and writhed through the shadows, I realized that I was an intruder in their domain. I honestly thought I was in the middle of a vivid and very real seeming nightmare or that perhaps I had fallen and bumped my head. This couldn't be real, at least that's what I was thinking. Fear surged through me as I tried to retreat, to find my way back to the path I had strayed from. But it was as though the forest itself had conspired to disorient me, to lead me further into its depths. The creatures were aware of my presence, their glowing eyes fixing on me with a predatory hunger. They moved closer, their movements synchronized like a macabre dance. I was their prey, and there seemed to be no way to escape. Desperation clawed at me as I tried to evade the creatures, to find a way out of this living nightmare. But the forest seemed to twist and contort, leading me further into the heart of the darkness. I was a prisoner in this dimension, a witness to the unspeakable horrors that lurked in the shadows. I don't know how I knew I had entered another dimension. There wasn't the internet and people just didn't discuss such things back then but it's like the knowledge of where I was suddenly hit me and I was stricken with fear, terror and grief at the thought that I might not ever find my way out of there.

The air was thick with a sickly, acrid scent, and a palpable sense of malevolence hung in the air. I was aware of the other lost souls who wandered through the nightmarish realm. They were as trapped as I was, their cries of despair echoing through the night. The creatures were relentless in their pursuit, their eyes glowing with an insatiable hunger. They were incredibly graceful yet somehow also they were clumsy and slow. I don't know how else to explain it but I could feel their malevolence, their desire to capture me and make me one of their own. I was their prey, and there was no escape from their clutches. I continued to stumble through the darkness, my heart pounding, my mind reeling with fear and confusion. The creatures closed in on me, their inhuman forms writhing and contorting with a terrible hunger. I was a stranger in a land of nightmares, and there was no escape from the horrors that lurked in the shadows. The forest seemed to stretch on endlessly, its darkness and malevolence unyielding. I had entered a portal to a dimension of unspeakable horrors, a realm of nightmares made flesh. I was a witness to the terrors that lurked in the shadows, a prisoner in a place that defied all logic and reason. As I ran for my life in a desperate attempt to escape, I thought that I would never escape this nightmarish realm. The creatures closed in on me, their eyes glowing with an unholy light. I was a stranger in a land of nightmares, and there was no escape from the horrors that lurked in the shadows. The forest seemed to stretch on endlessly, its darkness and malevolence unyielding. I had entered a portal to a dimension of unspeakable horrors, a realm of nightmares made flesh. I was a witness to the terrors that lurked in the shadows, a prisoner in a place that defied all logic and reason. Desperation gnawed at me as I tried to evade the creatures, to find a way out of this living nightmare. But the forest seemed to twist and contort, leading me further into the heart of the darkness. I was a prisoner in this dimension, a witness to the unspeakable horrors that lurked in the shadows, that were appearing and then transforming right in front of me, before my very eyes.

My fear was overwhelming, but I knew that giving in to despair was not an option. I had to find a way out of this living nightmare, a way back to the world I had known. I pressed forward through the suffocating darkness, my heart pounding and my mind filled with dread. The malevolent forest seemed determined to ensnare me, its branches and roots reaching out to pull me deeper into the shadows. But just as I thought all hope was lost, a faint, pulsating light appeared in the distance. It was a flicker of hope, a glimmer of salvation in the midst of the abyss. I stumbled toward it, my pace quickening as the light drew closer. As I reached the source of the light, it began to envelop me, wrapping me in a warm, comforting embrace. The grotesque creatures recoiled from its brilliance; their terrible hunger quenched by its radiance. I heard the monster's inhuman screams and howls in the background, slowly fading into oblivion as an invisible or maybe it was an ethereal barrier that separated me from them once again. With each step I took towards the light, the world around me began to unravel. The twisted landscape, the nightmarish creatures, and the oppressive darkness all melted away, like a nightmare fading with the dawn. Suddenly, I found myself back in the familiar woods near my house. The moon still shone high in the night sky, casting a silvery glow on the tranquil lake. It was as though I had never left, as though the nightmarish ordeal had been nothing more than a terrifying dream.

I collapsed to my knees, overwhelmed with relief. I had returned to the world I knew, escaping the clutches of the malevolent dimension. But the memory of the horrors I had witnessed would forever haunt my dreams, a reminder that there are realms beyond our understanding, where terrors lurk in the shadows. As I made my way back to my campsite, I couldn't shake the feeling that the portal I had stumbled upon was still out there, waiting to ensnare the unwary. I knew that I had been fortunate to escape with my life, but I also knew that others might not be so lucky.

The experience had left me with a profound sense of awe and dread, a realization that the boundaries of our reality are not as fixed as we might believe. In the darkness of that night, I had glimpsed a world of unspeakable horrors, a realm that defied all logic and reason. I could only hope that the portal to that nightmarish dimension remained hidden, forever out of reach. But in the stillness of the woods, I couldn't escape the feeling that something malevolent was still lurking in the shadows, waiting for its next victim.

With a heavy heart and a newfound awareness of the mysteries that lay beyond our understanding, I continued making my way back to my campsite, determined to leave behind the terrors of that night and to cherish the simple, comforting beauty of the world I knew. My mind immediately started trying to protect me by making up ways in which what had just happened to me had actually not happened. It was trying to convince me I had imagined all of it and right from the beginning I knew that I would never tell another soul about it unless it was absolutely necessary, which to this very day has never happened. And so, as I finally settled back into my campsite, staring off towards the tranquil lake and almost mesmerized by the silvery moon above, I knew that the memories of that night would never truly fade. The nightmares that had become reality in that malevolent dimension would forever haunt my dreams, a reminder of the inexplicable and the terrifying that lurked in the shadows of our world. I took a deep breath, grateful for my return to the familiar woods and the comforting embrace of the night. But the knowledge of what lay beyond, in the realm of nightmares made flesh, would forever linger in the depths of my consciousness, a reminder that our reality is not as certain as we might believe. The night remained silent, and I couldn't escape the feeling that somewhere in the distance, the portal to that nightmarish dimension still awaited its next unwitting traveler, ready to ensnare them in a world of unspeakable horrors. With a whole new sense, a newfound sense of vulnerability, I settled in for the rest of the night, the memories of that harrowing ordeal etched into my very soul.

Of course, I had nightmares all that night and I kept waking up in a cold sweat thinking that I was once again in that nightmare realm with those grotesque creatures. I thought I was losing my mind and once the sun rose the next day I left and never looked back. Something had changed inside of me but it's so lonely because I knew that I couldn't tell anyone and that no one would ever believe me about any of it. I actually feel uncomfortable even writing about it now but thought that I would give it a shot. Maybe there are other people out there who have experienced something similar or who knows, maybe there are those who've experienced the exact same thing. Sometimes it's all so clear in my mind and then other times it's jumbled up and twisted, as though my mind is trying to protect me from the worst of it. I also often wonder if there's things I don't remember, like when someone gets abducted and there's said to be a screen memory that's implanted, to keep them from remembering things they aren't supposed to or that they aren't ready for. I don't know but thank you for letting me share my story and maybe one day I will gather the courage to go back there and search for the portal again, this time armed with more knowledge than before and maybe even a way to prove the experience itself.

Eight
The Colorado Cabin

I grew up in Southern California and as a kid and young adult I don't think anything could have been better than living there. I was born in the sixties and enjoyed the sun and surf just as much as my peers always did. I still live there and have never moved but in the eighties I was going through some tough times and needed to get away. I wanted something different and I don't know if it was some sort of mid-life crisis or what but I decided to leave behind the sandy beaches and constantly sunny and cheerful weather and head to colder climates. Also, my work kept me incredibly busy. I work from home, I'm a writer, and the area where I lived wasn't the best and there was a lot of crime. Why am I telling you this? To give you an idea of how clueless I really was and to help you understand how I truly had no idea what I was getting myself into. I don't know how I ended up choosing Colorado, I think at the time it was just the most opposite to California a person could get, at least in my mind. Luckily I could take my work with me and decided to spend a little time in solitude in a remote cabin I rented. I had to look in the yellow pages to find a rental but eventually I did and that's what initially led me there. Sometimes I think the idea was implanted into my head by forces beyond the realm of my comprehension and understanding but the trip to the cabin in the heart of Colorado was meant to be a much-needed escape from the hustle and bustle of city life. I just wanted to get away and leave behind all of my problems and all of the problems in the city for a little while. I had no idea how profoundly it would change my life and that I would still think about it every day for all of these years. I longed for solitude, for a break from the daily grind. But as the days turned to weeks, and the cabin transformed into my sanctuary, I found myself isolated in the middle of nowhere, cut off from the outside world by an unrelenting blizzard.

The cabin itself was a rustic haven, perched on the edge of a snow-covered forest. Tall pines surrounded it, their branches heavy with the weight of the fresh snowfall. The blizzard had arrived with an unexpected fury, leaving me trapped inside, with no means of escape. My initial excitement at the prospect of a snowy retreat had turned to unease as the days stretched on. The solitude was oppressive, the silence broken only by the howling of the wind and the creaking of the cabin's timbers. I spent my time reading, gazing out at the snow-covered landscape, and occasionally venturing out to clear the paths. As I said, I had no idea what I was getting into, in more ways than one. I expected there to be snow, that was part of the point and what I was looking for, but I also expected to be able to leave and explore, to go places and possibly meet people. However, I was trapped there and I managed to catch writer's block of all things which had the exact opposite effect than what I had planned on happening once I was there and had gotten my wish. The nights were the worst. I would constantly glimpse shadows outside of the windows and while sitting in the living room watching television. I mostly saw them moving around out of the corner of my eyes and near the door to the large glass door that slid open to a large deck area. The cabin had no yard, in that the yard was the forest and it almost seemed, at least once night fell, that someone had dropped me in the middle of the woods and left me with no way of escaping. I thought I was losing my mind. The strange noises didn't help and one night I went out onto the deck to see what the hell was going on when I kept glimpsing something almost pacing back and forth on the deck and hearing strange scratching sounds back there as well. The glass had scratch marks etched into it that I knew for a fact hadn't been there before that.

I was scared and curious but I was also agitated. I thought it was some sort of wild animal and one night I had enough and yelled for it to show itself. I knew it was ridiculous and that a wild animal wasn't going to respond to me or approach me but I was exasperated and had literally come down with cabin fever. I needed to get out. It started with me walking out further into the woods during the daytime. It was beautiful and I started to become endeared to the idea of the cabin again. The fresh air and the snow- something I had only seen in movies up to that point- were so incredibly refreshing and invigorating. I finally started writing again and eventually I ventured out into the forest at night. It wasn't because I really wanted to but more like I didn't have a choice. I felt like I was being lured by whatever was out there. Whatever animal or creature had scratched up the glass sliding doors and that had been almost haunting me from outside in the woods since the moment I got there. It was on one of these forays into the biting cold, late at night and armed with only a flashlight, that I first caught a glimpse of the creature. It was while I was walking along the usual trail I had been taking and wearing down and while I was deep in thought, that I saw it out of the corner of my eye—a shadowy figure, lurking in the forest. It wasn't unlike the shadows I saw zipping past and pacing back and forth out of my peripheral vision almost for the entirety of the time I had been there. I stopped dead in my tracks and fear immediately and inexplicably gripped me. I made sure I had my flashlight on and tightly in my grip. My heart raced as I turned to get a better look, but the creature had disappeared. It left me with an unsettling feeling, a sense that I was not alone in this isolated wilderness. I had heard stories from the locals about strange happenings in the woods, tales of supernatural beings that roamed the area. I had always dismissed them as folklore, but now, in the midst of the blizzard, those stories took on a new, haunting significance. I couldn't explain it, the feelings I was having or why I felt the way that I did, but I just somehow knew that something supernatural was happening and that for whatever reason I had been the one chosen to see it. I mean, there was a part of my mind that thought it was my overactive writer's imagination but the primal feelings inside of my very soul told me differently. I turned and walked as quickly as I could back to the cabin and locked all the doors and windows behind me.

As the days wore on, the sense of unease only grew. The cabin seemed to creak and groan in the wind, its walls offering little comfort from the relentless storm outside. It was as if the very forest itself was alive, and I was an intruder in its domain. One evening, as I sat by the fire, I heard the creature again. This time, it was closer, and I could hear the soft, eerie sound of its movements in the snow. It was as if it was circling the cabin, its presence lurking just beyond what was my ability to see. I tried to remain calm and to tell myself that it wasn't necessary for me to have all the answers. There was also a curiosity in me that kept nagging at the back of my mind too. I would also be lying if I wasn't thinking about writing a fictional story around the events that were unfolding for me, as a part of my next book. All of those things and so many more ran through my mind all at once and as I continued to try and see what I was dealing with. I was hoping that before I went out to confront and try to scare off whatever was out there, that I would at least be able to see what it actually was that I was dealing with. I didn't have any weapons on me because I didn't know any better. Finally, I honestly felt like I was being taunted and had had enough of the whole situation. Fear coursed through me as I grabbed a flashlight and headed for the door. I needed to know what was out there, to confront the unknown. The snow crunched beneath my boots as I ventured into the cold night. The forest was a maze of shadows and darkness, the snow-covered trees looming like silent sentinels. I followed the sound of the creature's movements, my heart pounding in my chest. The beam of my flashlight swept across the snow, revealing odd footprints that led deeper into the woods. The snow had covered all of my footprints from several nights before when I had last been out there and had allowed myself to be scared off by whatever it was I was now chasing and planning on confronting. I knew they weren't my footprints; they weren't like any animal I had ever heard of or seen, not that I was any type of expert. They weren't human, that was obvious, but something inside of me told me they weren't exactly those of an animal either. Again, that strange suspicion of something supernatural happening all around me flooded my senses. I examined the prints more closely.

The prints were unlike any I had ever seen—large, with claw-like markings at the tips. They were spaced far apart, and their sheer size sent a chill down my spine. There was no denying it; something unnatural was lurking in the forest. I followed the tracks deeper into the woods, my breath forming puffs of vapor in the frigid air. The further I ventured, the more the forest closed in around me. The trees seemed to whisper with an otherworldly language, and my sense of dread was becoming almost overwhelming. It was then that I saw it—the creature, with fur matted with snow, standing in a clearing. It was massive, a hulking, shadowy figure that seemed to blend seamlessly with the night. Its eyes glowed with an eerie light, and I knew that I was in the presence of something not of this world. The creature let out a low, guttural growl, and I knew I had pushed too far. Panic surged through me as I turned and fled, the creature's growls echoing in the darkness behind me. I followed the strange footprints back to the cabin, my heart pounding, and my mind racing with fear. Back in the safety of the cabin, I locked the door and barricaded myself in. The creature remained outside, a dark and mysterious presence in the snow-covered forest. I knew I had encountered something that defied explanation, something that was far beyond the realm of the natural world. The blizzard continued to rage outside, and I was left with the unsettling knowledge that I was not alone in the wilderness. The cabin had become a sanctuary, but it was a fragile one, and the creature still lurked in the shadows of the forest.

I kept picturing it over and over again in my head. The matted gray fur, long and dirt stained even despite being covered in snow and sopping wet. The claws that looked more like talons on both the feet and the ends of the arms. The thing was huge! It had to have been twelve feet tall and it stood like a human being but it had the fur and face of a wolf. The snout especially. I had nightmares the next two nights and finally I couldn't take anymore. It had made its presence known, pacing on the back deck of the cabin but leaving prints this time. It would make low, guttural noises outside of my bedroom window all hours of the night. I packed my things three days before I had planned on leaving and I called a taxicab to get me out of there. The state of emergency was lifted and vehicles were allowed on the road again. I was sure to leave during the middle of the day to make sure there was no chance the creature was still lurking around out there, lying in wait for me to leave the cabin again. I saw footprints and followed them all around the cabin and some of them veered off and landed behind several trees nearest to the cabin, as if it were hiding behind the trees and peeking out, trying to catch me by surprise. I have thought about this at length for all of these years and I honestly don't know what kept it from just breaking the door down and coming in or smashing through the glass on the windows or the same door on the deck it had clawed. Are there some supernatural laws it has to follow and if so who makes them and what are they? I don't know but whatever the reason, I'm sure glad for it because that thing could have ripped me apart with its bare hands and used my largest bone as a mere toothpick. I never went to Colorado again and learned to appreciate the sand and surf again. Thanks for letting me share my story.

NINE
IN THE DEPTHS

I was sixteen years old when something extremely strange happened to me. I still struggle with it all these years later and whenever I remember the incident I feel like I am inside of a living nightmare. I figured writing it down and finally getting it off my chest and out into the world might help me overcome some of the terror I still feel. I grew up very sheltered in a rural and isolated area of Florida and I wasn't really allowed to hang out with friends or do anything on school nights with anyone but my siblings. One Friday night, all of my friends were going to a school dance and then to the beach the next day but of course I wasn't allowed to go. I was extremely upset. It was mainly my dad who had the issue with my going but he put his foot down, so to speak, and refused to even listen to the compromises my mother and I were trying to come up with. I was a normal teenager and hated the world that night. I didn't want to be around my family or my siblings, so my mother, in her infinite compassion, offered to allow me to camp out at the lake behind our house, located inside of a very dense and beautiful forest, all by myself. I think she was trying to give me some time to myself to cool off and also, even though I had been to that lake hundreds of times and had camped there just as much, I had never been able to do it alone before. I think she was trying to give me whatever freedom she could, remembering herself what it was like to be a sixteen year old girl. It was 1997, and I was headed out to a very familiar area near my house, nestled within the woods that surrounded a serene lake. It had always been a place of solace, a refuge from the demands of everyday life and the trauma of living with my controlling and overbearing father. My bond with this natural haven was strong, as I had camped by the lake and swum in its waters countless times, always with my siblings and always without any issue. We always had so much fun out there, no matter what we were doing, as the forest was huge and full of places to explore beyond the lake and the spot where we would all go fishing. But on this particular night, something eerie and unsettling would shatter the tranquility I had come to cherish.

I was different from everyone in my family, aside from maybe my mother, because I had always been drawn to the mysteries of the night, the secrets that it concealed under its cloak of darkness. The moon hung high in the sky, casting a silvery glow on the calm waters of the lake. The night was warm, inviting, and it beckoned me to venture beyond the confines of my tent. Again, that was nothing unusual. Sure, I had only ever explored further than the lake during the daylight hours or with one or all of my siblings if it were nighttime, but something was drawing me in out there, something I couldn't quite put my finger on. With how sheltered I was I think one would imagine I would be scared or at least a little bit uncomfortable with the idea of being out there, in that huge forest, all alone and in the dark. However, it was just the opposite and I felt almost compelled to explore a little bit. I walked all around the lake and beyond it and I was out there for about an hour. Eventually I started to feel strange and like I had ventured too far and had reached a place I wasn't supposed to be. I felt like I was being watched and possibly followed and only then did the fear I had expected earlier start nagging at the back of my mind. I hastily made my way out of the dense part of the forest and into the little clearing where the lake was. The lake wasn't little by any means and the depths of it were unknown to me. There was only so far I could go while still standing on my feet and I had been told many times by my father that it went extremely deep, though he never told me exactly how far down it went. I hustled back into my tent but almost immediately I felt foolish and reminded myself I was out there to let loose and have a little fun. I decided to strip off my clothes and go for a night swim in the lake. It was warm that night and I knew the water would be refreshing and not too cold.

As I stepped out into the crisp night air, my eyes were drawn to an eerie glow coming from the direction of the lake. It was an unnatural hue, a sickly green that seemed to pulse with a strange energy. A shiver ran down my spine, but curiosity overcame my initial unease. I moved closer to the lake, drawn by the eerie radiance that danced on the water's surface. The glow was concentrated in one specific area, as if something lurked deep beneath the tranquil surface. It cast an eerie, phosphorescent light on the surrounding trees, turning the night into an otherworldly spectacle. I stood stone still for a moment right on the shore, overwhelmed and terrified at what I was seeing. So many thoughts ran through my head in those first moments and I seriously contemplated just turning and running right out of the woods. I would leave my belongings behind and go out there again with my brother the next day, while the sun was in the sky, and gather them. It's like my mind and body were fighting one another with my body wanting nothing more than to do just that, to turn and run, but with my mind being drawn even deeper into the light underneath the lake. I didn't know much about extraterrestrials so that wasn't the first explanation that occurred to me and honestly I had been trying to convince myself it was some sort of natural phenomenon that my siblings and I just somehow seemed to miss every single time we had ever been out there overnight or that was something new that had sprung up since the last time we had been there. One way or another, there was something inside of me that was keeping me there and I wasn't able to bring myself to run away. The water emitted a soft, ominous hum, and ripples spread across the lake's surface, moving outward from the source of the glow. It was as if an unseen force stirred the waters, creating a palpable sense of tension in the air. Despite my growing trepidation, a strange compulsion overcame me, and I decided to take a nighttime swim in the mysterious waters. The eerie glow cast an ethereal quality over the lake, drawing me into its depths. I waded into the water, my body shivering with a mixture of fear and anticipation.

The glow grew more intense as I ventured and swam further from the shore. The water around me seemed to come alive, pulsating with an otherworldly energy. The surface of the lake trembled, and I felt an unseen presence beneath me, a force that tugged at my limbs, trying to pull me deeper into the water. I looked down but couldn't see anything in the dark water and I tried to kick it away but it had really latched on to me by that time. It was like almost immediately when I got to the point where I could no longer stand, something grabbed me. I didn't know what to think and my thoughts were all a jumbled mess anyway. I was terrified and screaming, doing everything in my power to get it to let go of me. It was no use. Panic surged through me as something unknown and malevolent tried to drag me into the depths, its grip strong and relentless. I kept fighting for what seemed like an eternity against the invisible force, kicking and thrashing in a desperate bid to break free. Finally, with a burst of strength, I managed to break the surface and scramble back to the safety of the shore. My heart pounded in my chest as I gasped for breath, my body covered in cold sweat. I was shaken, but I had escaped the clutches of the unknown, the eerie glow of the lake fading into the distance. I had been pulled even further from the shore by the unseen hands of whatever was under that lake. I sensed its presence following me until I got back to where I was able to stand and walk out of the lake. Once I reached that point though I didn't walk at all. I ran as fast as I could out of there and collapsed on the beach itself. I was exhausted for some reason as if whatever had a hold of me had somehow drained me of all of my energy. I must have passed out from the shock of it all or for whatever reason because I don't even remember blinking before I was waking up and it was morning. The sun beamed down onto me and when I opened my eyes it took me several minutes for my eyes to adjust to the brightness. I crawled back to my tent and slept some more. I woke up just as the sun was about to set and I was almost devastated that I wouldn't have time to pack up my things and get out of there before darkness fell completely. I kept looking back at the lake and then peeking out at it from my tent. There was nothing during the daytime that gave away that there was anything in there at all, let alone anything sinister or deadly.

I slept some more and I woke up in the middle of the night to use the bathroom. Once again I had almost no energy and I dreaded having to leave what I felt was at least the relative safety of my tent. I looked immediately to the lake and saw the same eerie glow from the night before. I walked to go and do my business, did it, and then went immediately back to my tent without so much as a glance towards the lake again. I woke up on Sunday feeling better than I had felt in a long time. I was still traumatized from the ordeal but that was how it was continuing to affect me mentally. Physically I felt refreshed and renewed. I packed everything up and again, without so much as a glance backwards, I went home. That's when I noticed hadn't escaped the whole ordeal as freely as I originally thought I had. The ordeal left its mark on me, both mentally and physically, or so it turned out. When I inspected my legs, I discovered strange, burn-like marks in the shape of what looked to be some sort of alien hand. They were painful and unsettling, a physical reminder of the eerie encounter in the depths of the lake. I told my older brother about it but swore him to secrecy otherwise and the next weekend we went out there at night. We weren't planning on camping but he had believed me and was desperate to see what was out there. Returning to my campsite, I could not shake the feeling of dread that clung to me. The events of that night were etched in my memory, a chilling reminder of the unknown terrors that lurk in the darkest corners of the world. The eerie glow of the lake, the unseen force that had tried to claim me, and the bizarre marks on my legs were mysteries that I could never fully explain. As we stood there on the edge of the shoreline, I knew that the events of that night would stay with me for the rest of my life. The eerie encounter in the depths of the lake was a secret I could never fully share or comprehend. It was a testament to the mysteries that remain hidden in the depths of the universe, a reminder that we are but small inhabitants in a world filled with enigmatic wonders and terrors.

TEN
UNDER SHAWNEE

I was on a solo vacation in Illinois visiting some family that I hadn't seen in a while when the thought occurred to me to go camping at Shawnee National Forest. My niece, who was one of the people I was there visiting in the first place, had mentioned a school field trip she had taken there recently and I thought it sounded fun. I asked several members of my family to join me but they all either had work or school, or they plain didn't want to go with me, and so that's how I ended up there alone. I didn't mind and actually I preferred it that way. I was always crisscrossing the country, whenever I had the time, and visiting national sights or camping alone in some random woodlands. Though, at the time I went to Shawnee, there weren't too many known places I hadn't been to yet, at least as far as I knew. But Shawnee was one of the places I hadn't visited yet and that made it all the more exciting. I should mention here that I am and always have been a firm believer in the paranormal and I've had more than a few odd and strange, sometimes downright supernatural, experiences while out on the road and in the woods in general. However, I never expected what happened to me to happen, and though it didn't deter me from continuing to explore campgrounds and forests all over the United States, it did make it so I was armed from then on when I did so and I trained myself to use a firearm.

The drive to Shawnee didn't take as long as I expected and I made good time. As I initially trekked through the forest I saw more people than I thought that I would and I was discouraged at first that maybe I wouldn't feel as alone as I would have liked. However, the further I walked into the woods, the fewer people I saw and eventually, the wonderful feeling of being completely isolated from other human beings and the rest of the world that I loved so much returned. I set up my camp very far away, at least as far as I knew, from anyone else and their campsites. As the sun dipped below the horizon, painting the sky in shades of deep orange and violet, I found myself in the heart of the Shawnee National Forest. A place known for its serene beauty, the forest took on an eerie and unsettling atmosphere as the last vestiges of daylight faded into the inky blackness of night. My decision to camp here, and not in one of the many other places that had been suggested to me by friends and my family, wasn't just due to my niece and her field trip. It had also been motivated by a longing for solitude, a break from the relentless chaos of daily life. I heard it was completely isolated and that even if there were other people around in the forest, it was more than likely that I wouldn't see them, and even if I did, I would still be able to find a spot all alone. I felt like I was in the middle of nowhere and the rest of the world didn't exist anymore, which was the plan in the first place. I was content and happy to be alive. The woods always gave me that feeling, you know? It somewhat makes a person feel like all of their problems are small, compared to the vastness of the forest itself. I don't know, maybe that sounds weird, but it's just how I feel, anyway. I sat by the flickering campfire, the only source of light and warmth in the encroaching darkness. A sense of peace washed over me as I gazed into the dancing flames, listening to the crackling of burning wood. I at least felt like I was alone in the forest, and that solitude was a cherished escape from the bustling world.

As the night wore on, a restless energy gnawed at me. I couldn't resist the lure of the dark woods beyond, and the temptation to explore the unknown pulled me from my campsite. That wasn't unusual and honestly that's how I had managed to have so many strange and sometimes supernatural experiences. Something about the darkness of the forest drew me in. It was something I always did, explored the forest as much as I could and under the cover of darkness. I thought the strange feelings washing over me all of the sudden were indicative that I would see some sort of apparition or perhaps a shadow being or two, as was normally the case when I felt that way. It got to the point where I was more fascinated than fearful, even though in the early years of the millennium no one ever spoke about such things as nonchalantly as I did and as I felt about them. It just was what it was, I guess. One thing I will say though is that nothing in the world could have prepared me for what was actually about to happen or what I was about to see. It ended up being the stuff of nightmares, and even though the shadow beings and phantoms had started off that way too, I knew within the depths of my soul that this experience would never become insignificant or run of the mill as the others had. I continued on my walk as the full moon cast an ethereal glow on the forest floor, its silvery light illuminating a path through the dense undergrowth. I ventured deeper into the forest, the shadows closing in around me. The silence of the night was oppressive, and the only sounds were my own footsteps and the gentle rustle of leaves underfoot. The thought of the vast, impenetrable darkness was enough to send shivers down my spine, but I couldn't resist the urge to continue. As I walked, I became aware of faint, strange noises that seemed to echo through the trees. It was an eerie chorus of whispers, almost like the muffled voices of countless spirits. My heart quickened, and my mind raced to explain the source of these unsettling sounds. It couldn't be anything other than the wind playing tricks on me, I assured myself. But the voices persisted, growing louder and more distinct. They seemed to be coming from a specific direction, drawing me closer to their source. A strange mixture of curiosity and dread overcame me, and I followed the eerie sounds deeper into the forest.

The whispers led me to a secluded part of the woods, where I stumbled upon a peculiar sight—an entrance to an underground tunnel. The tunnel's opening was a dark, gaping maw in the earth, and a cold draft emanated from its depths. This was nothing like something an animal could have dug and when I peeked inside it seemed to be an intricate and sophisticated tunnel system. It was probably left over from some forgotten time and I wondered if the people who owned the forest or those in charge of things such as field trips were even aware of its existence. It looked, somehow and in a way I can't quite explain, like it had only recently been opened up again. I got goosebumps all over my body and I stopped to listen. The strange noises were now emanating from within, echoing out into the night. I felt an irresistible compulsion to venture inside, to uncover the source of the eerie sounds. The tunnel was narrow and claustrophobic, its walls damp and cold to the touch. My flashlight flickered to life, casting a feeble beam into the inky blackness ahead. I swallowed hard, my heart pounding in my chest, and took my first cautious steps into the unknown. As I moved deeper into the tunnel, the whispers grew louder and more distinct, as if they were guiding me. The air grew colder, and the ground beneath my feet was slick with moisture. It was an ancient and forgotten place, and I couldn't help but wonder about the stories this tunnel held. The tunnel twisted and turned, its walls adorned with strange, indecipherable symbols and markings. It was as if I had stumbled upon an underground labyrinth, a place that had long been concealed from the world above. The echoes of the whispers reverberated through the subterranean passages, creating an eerie, unsettling ambiance.

My anxiety and curiosity battled within me as I continued to delve deeper into the tunnel. The light from my flashlight revealed more cryptic symbols etched into the walls, along with strange drawings that resembled grotesque, ghoulish figures. It was an unsettling sight, and I couldn't shake the feeling that I was intruding on something ancient and forbidden. Then, as I rounded a corner, I was met with a sight that sent a chill down my spine. In a small chamber off to the side, I saw the source of the whispers—a cluster of shadowy figures. They were huddled together, their forms distorted and grotesque, their eyes gleaming with an eerie, malevolent light. They weren't anything like the "usual" shadow beings I had seen so many times in the middle of the night in woods all over the country before. Those things were made of shadow and were darker than the darkness of the night. What I was looking at right then, in that tunnel and in those moments, weren't made of shadow and had substance to them. I knew they were some sort of hideous creatures and I wasn't sure I wanted to know what they looked like. In the end and once again my curiosity got the better of me and I tried, but I couldn't make out their features. Regardless of that, the air was heavy with a palpable sense of dread. The creatures seemed to be conversing in hushed tones, their voices a dissonant chorus of eerie, unworldly sounds. I didn't understand what they were saying. The language they were speaking sounded almost like a garbled form of the English language as some words sounded familiar, but not entirely. There was also a strange echo to their voices of which I can't explain. My presence had not gone unnoticed, and the figures turned their unnerving gazes toward me. Panic surged through me, and I stumbled back, my flashlight trembling in my hand. The unearthly beings began to advance, their movements jerky and unnatural. I knew I had to escape, to retreat from this subterranean nightmare, but the tunnel seemed like it had grown labyrinthine, and I was disoriented, lost in the ancient depths. As I desperately navigated the winding passages, the whispers of the creatures grew louder, their dreadful, cacophonous voices reverberating in the confined space. My flashlight flickered, casting long, grotesque shadows that danced on the tunnel walls. I was trapped in a nightmare, a place of darkness and despair. Then, as if in response to my unspoken prayers, I stumbled upon a faint, distant glimmer of moonlight. With renewed determination, I pushed forward, following the faint light to the tunnel's entrance. The cold night air was a welcome relief, and I burst from the tunnel's confines, gasping for breath.

I had escaped the underground horrors, but the unsettling presence of the ghoulish creatures remained etched in my memory. Their malevolence, the whispers in the dark, and the unearthly symbols in the tunnel haunted my thoughts. Returning to my campsite, I extinguished the campfire and retreated into my tent. I knew that I would never be able to avoid all predatory animals or whatever else was out there should I choose to abandon the forest altogether at that time to return to my vehicle and get out of there. I wanted to though and I think back now on how that makes no sense. I was more than willing, excited even, to explore the forest at night but not to leave after what I had seen. I think the creatures had something to do with that, maybe they were more supernatural than I had initially realized but that's just speculation on my part and I will never know the truth of what really kept me there. One thing is for sure though and that's that the events of that night left me with an overwhelming sense of dread and fear, a reminder of the unknown terrors that lurk in the darkest corners of the world. I knew I would never forget the eerie encounter in the underground tunnel, the whispers of the ghoulish creatures, and the inexplicable dread that clung to me. It was a night that had forever changed me, a night I would never fully escape, no matter how far I traveled from that dark and ancient forest.

———

CONTINUE WITH
BEYOND THE PATH: TRUE TALES OF TERROR
IN THE WOODS: VOLUME 2

ABOUT THE AUTHOR

Erik Lake, a pen name adopted to maintain privacy, is a seasoned author with a deeply-rooted passion for the mysteries of human culture and the unexplained. Prior to embarking on his writing career, he served as a professor of anthropology at a prestigious university, where he was celebrated for his captivating lectures and scholarly publications. His academic pursuits led him across the globe, from the jungles of the Amazon to the mountainous terrains of the Himalayas, in search of understanding the complexities of human behavior and tradition.

Throughout his academic tenure, Erik developed a keen interest in folklore, myths, and the stories that often go untold or are overshadowed by mainstream narratives. It was this curiosity that led him to explore themes of the paranormal and the enigmatic phenomena that challenge our understanding of reality.

Since leaving academia, Erik has devoted himself to full-time writing, specializing in works that merge his anthropological background with topics often considered too taboo or unsettling for conventional scholarly dialogue.

Erik Lake brings to the literary world a rare blend of academic rigor and open-minded curiosity. Whether he's shedding light on cryptids, spirits, or age-old legends, his works provide a well-balanced blend of skepticism and wonder, prompting readers to question their own beliefs and perspectives.

Away from the pen and paper, Erik enjoys hiking, amateur photography, and spending time with his family in a quaint, undisclosed location surrounded by nature's untamed beauty. Yet, the woods for him are not just a retreat but an ongoing field of research—a labyrinth of endless questions and bewildering phenomena that continue to fuel his prolific writing career.

ALSO BY FREE REIGN PUBLISHING